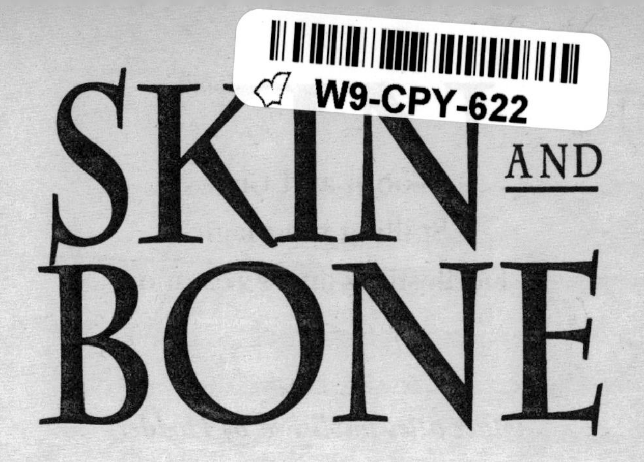

Stephen Moore lives in Newcastle upon Tyne with his wife and his young son.

SKIN AND BONE is the stunning sequel to widely acclaimed TOOTH AND CLAW, and his fourth novel for children. His first two, SPILLING THE MAGIC and FIDDLESTICKS AND FIRESTONES, are also published by Hodder Children's Books.

Also by Stephen Moore:

Tooth and Claw
Spilling the Magic
Fiddlesticks and Firestones

Other titles published by Hodder:

Owl Light
Dark of the Moon
Maggie Pearson

Bag of Bones
Helen Cresswell

Dolphin Luck
Hilary McKay

The Incredible Journey
Sheila Burnford

SKIN AND BONE

STEPHEN MOORE

a division of Hodder Headline plc

First published in Great Britain in 1998
by Hodder Children's Books

10 9 8 7 6 5 4 3 2 1

A Catalogue record for this book is available from the
British Library

ISBN 0340 70455 1

Typeset by
Palimpsest

Printed and bound in Great Britain by
Mackays of Chatham

Hodder Children's Books
A Division of Hodder Headline plc
338 Euston Road
London NW1 3BH

For Jenny, who is the real Bryna,
and Kim, who I grew up with.

Contents

PART ONE

One

Drought

Drought.

No winter snow. No spring thaw. No April showers or summer rain. A mountain lake become a puddle. A running river, baked dry all but a sliver.

Drought.

All things carried the scars of its passing.

A sky endlessly blue, relentlessly flat and cloudless. A brutal, hard white sun beating down day upon day without relief: nothing alive, nothing left whole beneath its pitiless stroke.

Drought.

In open countryside the summer grass stood stiff and brittle, and bleached white; or else was burned black where the sun's heat had been so intense it had erupted into swathing flame. Everywhere, tired trees held up their bare branches in protest to the sky. The few leaves that still clung to them were dry and twisted, and bristled and crackled when the wind blew.

Drought.

The empty buildings of the town, that had seemed for so long to be beyond change, stood sun-scorched. Paint peeled from doors and windows; in places dried-out timbers turned and snapped in their settings, showering the streets with broken glass. Steel warped. Concrete cracked. Walls bulged uneasily in the heat of the day.

Between the buildings, out on the streets, the roads blistered, their tar melted and ran together in dangerous, stinking-hot pools: liquid death to an unwary traveller.

The garden hedges, the public lawns, the wind-blown weeds upon the riverbanks, the open pastures of the Town Moor: they were all dead (or at best dying). And the great black-and-white gawp-eyed beasts, the bullocks that had for so long fed upon the Town Moor? Dead too. Their meat, what little there had been of it, had come as a welcome winter's feast to starving animals – the dwindling numbers of town cats and dogs who somehow survived there still.

All that was left of the cattle now was their scattered bones: to serve as a reminder of an endless, unsatisfied hunger, to serve as a reminder of . . .

Drought.

It was early evening. The sun still lingered in the sky, stood full and red above the far horizon as if it was reluctant to set; but at least the worst of its fierce heat had gone for the day. Blind Bryna walked slowly across the empty barren fields of the Town Moor. Let the unforgiving stone surface of a narrow, man-made road guide her paws as she moved downhill towards the riverside.

She was not alone. At one shoulder walked a large, black, heavy-boned she-cat, and at the other hobbled an equally large, three-legged, ginger tom. (From their stance and build it was obvious that Bryna's companions were brother and sister.)

Kin or not, all three cats showed the same tell-tale signs of near-starvation. Their tongues were swollen, their bruised eyes sat deep within their heads, their fur was dull and patched, their skin hung loose upon their bones. And they moved slowly, deliberately, each step carefully chosen so as not to waste their body strength needlessly.

"Must we drink from the river *so* close to the crossing, Bryna?" asked the tom, Ki-ya. "It will be well guarded. Surely, Dart could find us an easier spot farther upstream—?"

"Pah," spat Bryna, not letting him finish. "This is our prowl. This has always been our prowl. Why should we go out of our way to try and quench our thirst?"

"Aye," said the she-cat, Dart. "And anyway, there isn't a single stretch of water *not* bursting with foolish animals keen to do murder to keep it to themselves."

Ki-ya shook his head, sadly. "I'm only saying . . . It'll be dogs. And there'll likely be a fight."

"Aye, well, then it's more fool them," said Dart.

Bryna stood still a moment, lifted her nose; the slope of the hill had lessened beneath her paws and the slight, sweet, tantalising smell of running water came to her. They had come off the Moor and before them now, between lines of empty houses and heavy grey industrial buildings, was the river; what was left of it.

At the place of the crossing the fallen stones of a broken bridge stood high and dry off the river-bed. Once the river had hardly noticed the stones there as it rushed on by. Now, almost comically, a thin single thread of water struggled to find a way between them.

Ki-ya was right about the dogs. Quickly he counted eight: a mix of common mongrels lying carelessly in the dry dust at the edge of the river. And if they were more empty bags of bone than solid muscle, they were still full-grown animals; who did not bother to move themselves when the cats walked between them to reach the running water.

"You're not welcome here, moggy," growled some dog under his breath. There were howls of laughter, as if it was all some big joke, and eyes turned their way. But still the dogs did not move.

"Where else, but the river, would you have us quench a thirst?" said Dart, with a flick of her tail. "Doesn't water come free?"

"Aye, well, now that you come to mention it – it's not so free for some of us any more," said the dog. "Least ways, not for moggies!" Again there were howls of laughter.

"You cannot deny us a drink, brother," said Ki-ya, deliberately walking to the water's edge and stooping as if to take one.

"I am no brother of yours, cat. And I'll deny you whatever I like if you cannot pay for it." Suddenly the dogs were sitting up. They were large animals in spite of the obvious effects of the drought, and loomed over the cats. Tails among them were wagging. It was obviously a game they had played before, and they thought themselves clever at it.

"Pay for it?" spat Bryna. She lifted her nose to scent out the dogs; wanted to be certain of their positions in case they attacked.

"Times are hard if you hadn't noticed," said the dog, who by his bold stance was obviously the leader of their makeshift pack. "You'll get nowt for nowt here. So . . . What have you got in exchange for your drink of water? And if it's an empty bag of wind, then you can bugger off back to wherever it is you came from. Before we decide to take ourselves a piece of cat for breakfast."

"I'll give you bags of wind!" Dart's hackles lifted, she began to spit and pawed the ground with her open claws. Dogs began to growl, to bare their teeth.

"Not so fast, sister," said Ki-ya, "not so fast. Eight against three wouldn't exactly be a fair fight now, would it? And who would it serve to get into a fight? There's not one of us here – not a dog or a cat – with the body strength to heal an open wound."

The dog pack seemed to hesitate, and they fell silent. But the lead dog stood his ground, lifted his tail high, called Ki-ya's bluff.

"Nowt for nowt," he said again. "Nowt for nowt."

Bryna tried to move to one side of him, only to find him moving with her, blocking her way with his body. And the other dogs, less brave than their leader, fell in behind, copied him like shadows.

"Oh, I've had enough of all this nonsense," cried Dart. She lifted her claws and raked the first nose that came within her reach. Struck out again and again before the stricken animal had time to react. Had these dogs been seasoned fighters, then things might have gone badly for the cats in their weakened condition. Luckily the dogs were not. Full grown they might have been, but they were young still, and unpractised at the kill.

Suddenly the cats puffed up their fur and seemed to double in size. And they moved with such speed, surely there weren't just three of them now, but half a dozen at least!

The dogs turned and bolted without making a proper fight of it. Squealing as they ran like frightened pups.

And so at last, Bryna, Dart and Ki-ya took their drink of water and quenched their burning thirst. But there was no real pleasure in it. They sat uneasily together at the edge of the river, their bodies still nervously agitated, the kick of their breath heavy and uneven after their run-in with the dogs. Had their world become so bad they were reduced to fighting overgrown pups for a lap of water?

Not for the last time, blind Bryna's thoughts drifted back to a time, long ago, when men had walked the streets of the town. A time when, as a kit, she had been content to be the lazy lap-cat of a doddery old woman called Mrs Ida Tupps. She had lived in a house, been fed and watered on demand.

Then she remembered that long dark winter's night when mankind had abandoned the town, abandoning their pets with it; leaving them behind, without pity, to fend for themselves. She remembered the almost impossibly hard struggle to stay alive; and those dogs and cats who had learned to survive *together*. (Indeed, who, together in unity, defeated in battle the creature Dread Booga – the most vile of all their two-footed enemies.) And once truly free of men, they had lived as it pleased them to live. They had hunted side by side as equals. Whelped their kits and pups together. Did not fight each other for the spoils of territory. Did not kill each other for sport. And there had always been food enough to share, water from the river in abundance.

Ah, but this was all ancient history now . . .

Because then had come the drought. The endless, unforgiving drought, that could not be battled with, or run away from; that had crept upon them slowly, and bit by bit stolen away . . . *everything*. By day there was only the murdering sun and the sun-scorched wind. By night only the bitter cold of a cloudless starlit sky.

The changes in the behaviour of the cats and dogs came as slowly as the drought. At first it was just young kits and immature pups picking silly, mindless arguments with each other. Bad-tempered bickering and name-calling. But then the adults had begun to fight openly in the street. To kill even; and claim it as an act of self-defence.

Suddenly, animals were prowling warily, and seldom alone. They began to move about in huddles or family groups, often waiting for the relative safety of nightfall before venturing out in search of food.

As the drought worsened, the unrest spread. The huddles became more organised; formal gangs or packs with leaders and seconds; with formidable territories and uncrossable boundaries, to be envied and fought over. And the riverside, with its failing supply of water, was the most prized territory of all.

Older, wiser animals had tried to make the others see the foolishness of it, to see sense, but to no effect. No sensible animal was listening. Endless thirst, endless hunger, and bitter, selfish rivalry has a way of hardening the softest of hearts. Soon, even the oldest of allies had found themselves choosing opposite sides. The broken bones of the long dead, which still littered the streets from ancient battles, were easily forgotten beneath the growing piles of new.

The three cats were not left to themselves for long. A small group of animals suddenly appeared between the fallen stones of the bridge on the far side of the river. Cats this time; two pairs. Ki-ya looked wearily between Dart and Bryna. He did not have the body strength, or the spirit, to face another fight so soon.

As the newcomers approached, it became clear – for those with eyes to see – that these cats were in no better condition than they were themselves. Slow-moving, gaunt and empty-bellied. But there was something else about them; they were all exactly the same peculiar colour. A disturbing brown. Not the brown of natural fur, but a permanent stain from ground-in dirt. And if the strangeness of their colour was not enough to worry an animal, their bodies stank – reeked of some foul unnatural scent. Bryna, blind, did not see their approach. But she smelled them all right, and, odd though it might seem, their awful stench lifted her spirits and brought a gentle purr to her throat. You see, these were sewer cats, the last of their kind; animals who, up until the drought, had survived by hunting the rats that once thrived in great numbers in the drainage system beneath the town. (The vermin were all but gone now. The sewers had long run dry and become dangerous, often blocked, prone to sudden rock falls and cave-ins. Only its ancient smells lingered to remind a cat's nose.) Among these sewer cats came the oldest of Bryna's friends. A big, gangly tom called Treacle.

"Oh, B-Bryna, there you are. W-We've been looking all over for you," he began excitedly.

"All over, Captain," echoed Lugger, a smaller sharp-eyed tom who always stood at Treacle's side.

"You'll never guess what's happened—"

"Never guess, Captain—"

"Welcome stranger," interrupted Ki-ya, with mock formality, and a pinch of his nose.

"What? Oh, er, y-yes, yes, welcome stranger."

With that, all the cats were purring and cuffing each other playfully, rubbing heads and tails in a simple display of open-hearted affection.

"But now, now you must listen to me, Bryna," Treacle continued at last, when their welcome was done and a second, extravagant drink shared between them. "It's Kim . . . *Kim.* He has called a Council."

"A Council, Captain," echoed Lugger.

"The daft old dog has called a *Council*?" spat Dart. "But what on earth for? What animal will even bother to turn up these days?"

"It's a gathering for all animals who have a voice to speak or a leg to stand on," went on Treacle as if he had not heard Dart's rebuff. "Word has it, some cat's got himself an idea he wants to share—"

"Idea, Captain—"

"A way to save us from this awful drought."

"Save us, Captain—"

"Oh, is that all . . . an idea," said Dart, dipping her tongue into the thin trickle of river water.

"Yes, yes — and I told him you would all come. And I mean, I mean – you will come, won't you?"

"Won't you, Captain—?"

Blind Bryna lifted her nose to the sky, stood stock still. And in that moment felt a strange, unsettling coldness as the slightest of fleeting shadows passed across her body. Far away, a lone bird had flown across the face of the sun. Bryna shuddered with a sudden sense of deep foreboding. Why? She did not know, but the feeling of dread was real enough and would not pass away.

"Yes," she said, firmly, answering Treacle's question for them all. "Yes, we will come to the Council . . ."

Two

SKRINKLE

The huge bird spread his wings wide to take advantage of the steady up-draught. It was already early evening, but the grumbling air was still warm and rising around him, buffeting his flight feathers, lifting him higher and higher, until he soared freely upon the back of the perfect, clear blue sky.

Skrinkle – for that was his name – had flown a long way that day, far beyond the ranges of his own mark that lay within the shadows of the mountains, towards the setting sun. He had flown without rest, without taking his ever-watchful eyes from the ground far below him. He had marvelled at the vicious strength of the drought – surely, its talons had scar-marked the whole world! He had wondered at the great grey body of the town rising up before him out of the river valley, sudden and massive; with its seemingly endless lines of empty buildings; man-made mountains reaching out as if to capture the sky. And he had puzzled over the animals who prowled its streets still; the countless cats and dogs who, though they thirsted and starved, would not stray beyond its edges, as if cooped there like helpless chickens. Easy meat for such as himself . . .

Ah, but now he was coming home. He was exhausted and he was hungry; not for food, but for the company of his mate.

And then, there it was: his home mark. Where upland streams had once tumbled gaily down steep, lush green hillside, only brutal scars upon bare, stone-dry earth remained; but this place was his own, none-the-less.

He closed his wings momentarily, ducked his head, and swooped down through the sky in a long, slow circle. Ever-watchful he took in the run of the ground as he fell. Picked out the last patch of open heath still thick enough with stick-brittle scrub to cover his landing; and then, with a shrill, piercing cry of relief, he brought himself to ground.

And as Skrinkle-the-bird lands, watch him carefully.

As he stretches out his great wings one last time, and steadies himself with open talons, watch him *very* carefully; in case you should miss it.

Not two legs clawed, but four legs standing. Not ruffled feathers, but glossy fur. Not the bright yellow of a razor-sharp beak, but the stained yellow of grinning teeth and a lolloping tongue. Not Skrinkle-the-bird now, but Skrinkle-the-fox.

Not Skrinkle-the-bird now; Skrinkle-the-fox.

Weary with the effort of the flight, panting heavily for breath and exhausted by the sudden change that had come upon him, the fox fell heavily to the ground. He would be safe enough from prying eyes, hidden among the scrub, for the short time it took him to gather his strength and come back fully to his true self. And anyway, he was not alone—

Close by, long hidden in the undergrowth, a vixen lies in wait, discreetly watching over him . . .

Three

The Council

The moonlit night came bitterly cold. And while midnight stars snapped brightly against the blackest of skies, Bryna sat patiently upon the Town Moor. She had been waiting there a long time for the Council to begin. Sitting around her in a vague circle were, at most, twenty animals. More cats than dogs, but a desperately poor showing, considering the large numbers who still prowled the town. They had come in dribs and drabs, reluctant ones and twos, sitting uneasily together out in the open. Bryna sensed them all well enough. Their body smells: healthy or sick. The noises they made as they breathed. The taste they left upon her tongue. The way their movements agitated the freezing night air, tickling her whiskers, ruffling her fur. What use had she for eyes?

Closest to her sat Kim, an ancient black-haired mongrel dog, and in his shadow lay a sickly kit, name of Sleekit. Next came the two sewer cats, Treacle and Lugger, in the company of Ki-ya and Dart. Then a Labrador with her barely-weaned dog-pup: Fisher and Saal. And then a desperately thin-ribbed greyhound called Cherry, who was so highly-strung and agitated she could not stop whimpering or sit still in one place for more than a few moments at a time.

"Well, Kim, well—?" cried Cherry, suddenly unable to bear the silent wait any longer. "Are we just going to sit here all night, freezing our tails off? We've waited long enough. It's obvious no other animal is coming. Let's have this daft idea – then we can all go and find ourselves a warm den for the night."

There was a long moment of thoughtful, uneasy silence. The kit, Sleekit, scratched himself self-consciously. Kim farted, relieved his aching belly of the wind, and felt much better for it. (He was getting *far* too old for this kind of silly business.)

At last the old dog struggled to his feet, slowly turned himself about and looked down upon the town and the withered, desolate riverside framed by the harsh moonlight. Kim had been a respected leader of animals once. When he had barked, dogs and cats had come running; when he had used his teeth they had known they were bitten.

And now? He had called the Council personally . . . most animals had simply ignored him!

He pawed the ground in frustration, a deep growl rising in his throat. "Why did I bother? Why—? Take a look out there, my friends. Go on, take a look . . ." Heads turned self-consciously his way. "Can't you see the cats and dogs fighting each other? Can't you hear the killings made? The packs, the gangs, thieving from each other, murdering? Aye—! And over what? A few dry stretches of dead earth . . .

"And then there's the loners. Vicious thugs, saying it's every animal for themselves, claiming we're all fair game to a hungry mouth.

"Doing the drought's work for it, daft beggars. All of them — Doing the drought's work for it!"

No animal answered him. They all knew the truth of these matters, but they did not answer because they did not have an answer.

"What is he saying, mother?" asked the dog-pup, Saal, innocently enough. "Are we to be an army to fight against them?" All around the circle there were sniggers and derisory yowls of laughter. Even Bryna could not help joining in.

Kim growled impatiently, tried not to laugh with them. The time for armies was well past.

Their bodies were too weak and ailing. Their numbers far too few. Indeed, if the drought did not relent they would all be joining the dead, soon enough.

Once more the meeting fell into a frustrated silence. And sadly, before it broke, there were two or three extra gaps in their circle, where faint-hearted strangers had crept away into the darkness.

And then at last, from out of the night a new voice spoke. "I . . . I know what must be done," it said, boldly. "I know." It was the kit, Sleekit, who all this time had been lying quietly at Kim's side.

"Oh, you do, do you?" mocked Cherry.

"Let him speak!" growled Kim.

Sleekit stood up, walked boldly into the middle of the circle, determined to face his heckler on his own account. He was a young cat, though you might not have guessed it to look at him (the drought had seen to that). His body was a mixture of rough, tatted fur and ugly bald scabs, where old wounds, marks of deep infection and disease, had tried unsuccessfully to heal themselves.

"Tell me, Cherry," he said, quietly, "if you could wish for anything, anything at all, what would it be?"

"What! Is it kittish guessy-games, now?"

"Maybe so, friend. But tell us all anyway . . ." said Kim.

"All right, I'll play a little longer. I'll tell you what I want, what we all want, if it isn't blindingly obvious! — Food to fill a starving belly. Fresh water to quench a choking thirst. And, above all, we want a place to do it where our own kin does not pick a fight, does not try to make a meal out of *us* for the privilege!"

"Aye, aye . . ." cats and dogs began to mutter in agreement.

"But so much for wishes, kitten," mocked Cherry, "so much for dreams. Unless, of course, you're going to tell me there *is* such a place . . . ?"

"Have you forgotten so much already?" growled Kim. "Before the drought—"

"Pah! *Before* the drought—"

"Aye, Cherry, before the drought, this town was that very place!"

"Yes, well, it certainly isn't now, is it?" Cherry began to pace anxiously around the circle of animals. Setting cats' tails swinging, dogs growling.

"No," said Sleekit, at last. "No, Cherry, you are right. This town is not the place it once was . . . That is why I'm leaving it in search of another. And you must all come with me. In brotherhood, in sisterhood . . ."

All around him cats hissed hysterically, dogs growled deep in their throats.

"Leaving the town! *This* is your idea!" spat Dart, suddenly standing. "This is what we risked our lives to come and hear this night – the ranting of a kitten! Who's been filling your silly head with such nonsense?" She flicked her tail accusingly in Kim's direction.

"Surely, Sleekit, the buildings of this town are our bones. Its moors are our flesh. Its river is our blood," said Treacle, anxiously.

"Aye! Bones and blood, Captain," echoed Lugger.

"Or tell me it isn't so? Tell me we do not *belong* here?"

"Are you *really* asking us to prowl the wild countryside?" asked Ki-ya, solemnly. "Do you want us to take a deliberate walk with death upon the *Outlands?*"

"Walk with death? Can it be worse? Isn't this drought the very mother and father of death?" said Sleekit, as bravely as he could. "Yes, Ki-ya, I do want us to prowl the Outlands."

"What! If you were not the blood of my own womb, Sleekit, I would say you had gone mad." Suddenly it was Dart's tail that was swinging wildly and her paws scuffed the ground eager to find some young ear to box.

Ki-ya and Bryna could not stop an amused purr from rising to their throats. There was Dart, Sleekit's reluctant mother, freely admitting to their kinship. In truth it was an open secret, but who would have thought it? It had always seemed more likely that Bryna and Ki-ya would have paired, but Bryna was barren, a legacy of her time spent as a kit in the company of men; there could be no offspring from their union. No. Quite out of character, it was Dart who became the mother. In the early spring she had gone missing for a time, only to return, unabashed and secretive, and in the company of this thin, poorly-built kit she called Sleekit. She never took to him, or to motherhood in general. He was such a sickly kitten, clumsy at the hunt; a loner, a wanderer and a thinker. Who, when he needed companionship, preferred the slow company of the ageing dog, Kim, to his own kin. (Once, in private, Bryna had pressed Dart about Sleekit's father, but she had only spat and hissed and stalked off angrily. The subject was never mentioned again.)

It was Dart's hissing that silenced their purrs now. "Pah—! Well, I for one am not going to stay here and listen to any more of this nonsense!" She swung her tail at Sleekit, turned her backside into his face before stalking out of the Council.

"Dart—?" Bryna called after her, wanting to reason with her; and suddenly embarrassed, as if she was somehow personally responsible for Sleekit's wild idea.

"Pah!"

Ki-ya coughed politely, tried to break the tension, lolloped to his feet. "Sleekit, your mother, she does have a point, you know." With that he followed Dart out of the circle. Together, they moved some distance off, but in the event stayed deliberately within earshot: they weren't about to miss anything important.

The eyes of the Council fell upon Bryna

now. She could almost feel the weight of their stare.

"And will *you* walk out on me, Bryna?" asked Sleekit. Adding quickly, just in case she got the idea his resolve was weakening, "Because I mean to go into the Outlands whether you come or not. And I'm sure there are others here who will gladly follow."

There were more excited kittish mews and yowls of agreement.

In all honesty, Bryna was not sure how to answer. To go out into the wild countryside was not a new idea. Indeed, hadn't it even occurred to her at some time of crisis? But the madness soon passed. No animal born of the town had ever prowled beyond its edges; none who had ever returned again, that is. To the dog and the cat – even to Ki-ya and Dart, cats born as close to the wild as any moggy has a right to be – the town was the whole world. It was the limit of their territory, as is nature's way. And the wild countryside, the Outlands beyond? Just that . . . *Outlands.* Mysterious, dangerous, unknown and forbidden.

"Where you seek to go there are no buildings to give an animal shelter when he needs it," said Bryna, quietly. "No safe gardens to prowl, no protected moorland. And unknown dangers stalk there upon four legs, slide about upon their bellies with tongues of poison. Dangers we cannot even put a name to."

"Have you been there already, then?" asked Cherry, excitedly.

"Well, no, but—"

"Then how do you know about all these *so-called* dangers?"

Again there was a certain truth in the question that Bryna found hard to answer. How could Bryna know for sure? "Do the tales of our ancestors mean nothing to you? Or are your ears only open to the stories you want to hear?"

"Anything's got to be better than staying here," said Sleekit, his voice growing loud with anger. "I will not wait to die of thirst and starvation. I will not wait to be set upon and killed by some gang of crazed animals eager for the lickings of a puddle! Am I not a cat wild-born—?" He hesitated, looked quizzically around him.

At that, Treacle stood up at Sleekit's side. "Ha! Maybe this kit is more his mother's son than we give him credit for!"

"Mother's son, Captain," echoed Lugger.

"Aye, but you speak so freely of food and water, Sleekit," said Kim, cautiously. "*Is* there water to be found upon the Outlands? Now choose your words carefully, do not mock us."

"A direct path to it!" answered Sleekit, suddenly sure of himself.

"What *path* is it that finds its way to water?" mocked Cherry.

"Our own river, of course—!"

"Eh?"

"Isn't the river in drought the strangest of creatures? I have studied its ways . . . how often its waters rise to a thin trickle in one place, only to seep back into the river bed in another, leaving only damp muddy ground to remind us of our thirst. And how often the mud dries up, turns hard and brittle; baked as dry as any stone road."

"Aye, and don't we know it to our cost!" There was an outbreak of feeble laughter.

"Don't you understand my meaning yet?" cried Sleekit, desperate again.

"Aye, we understand the river water rises and the river water falls. So what?"

"So we must follow its dry course beyond the edges of the town, beyond the gangs that haunt it. Follow it until at last its waters rise again within the Outlands, as surely it must!"

"Must?" said Bryna. "Must? You know this for certain, kit?"

Sleekit fell silent, his feeble claws clutching the ground in desperation as he huddled there against the cold night. When at last he did speak again, his voice was weak and hesitant. "I will tell you what I know for certain, Bryna. I know . . . I know the dangers of this town. I know how the end will surely come to us all if we remain here. It is only a matter of time. What we don't know about the Outlands might yet be turned to our advantage. Or tell me it's not possible, if you can? Tell me it's not possible . . ."

Wasn't the whole world a madness? Stay where they were and sure enough they would all die; killed by the burnt breath of a sun-scorched wind; or just as likely slaughtered by their own kin. Or else prowl into the Outlands upon some wild quest and die together in the looking.

Again the Council fell into a deep, brooding silence. Again, more than a few wary animals crept out of their circle, melted away into the night.

In that silence blind Bryna sat strangely alert. Ears upright, sightless eyes staring. Her head began to ache. Vague shadows drifted across her mind, pressed in upon her with a growing weight that was almost too heavy to bear. And then, as clearly as if he was standing there in front of her, she saw him, and a peculiar sight: a huge tom cat with a smudged, charcoal-ginger fur, and one eye scarred a livid white. But even more oddly, perched on his shoulder was a small brown bird, a sparrow, happily chittering nonsense to itself.

Inside her head Bryna saw this cat clearly enough. More than that; she recognised him, knew him by name. Grundle he was called, Ki-ya's father, a wild-born cat . . .

A dead cat.

Aye, and long dead, too.

Grundle was one of Bryna's ghosts. In

her time she had often seen ghosts, it was nothing unusual, nothing to fear. And a cat does not need eyes to see ghosts. For her there was only joy in this meeting of old friends, and a thrumming purr lifted to her throat.

The ghost cat did not speak, but sat himself quietly at Bryna's side, within the ring of the Council. The reassuring weight of his presence was enough.

Bryna's mind was set; she knew in her heart that she must go with these foolish dogs and cats; she would leave the town and prowl the Outlands, though her tongue soured and her head ached anew at the thought of it.

There was one last argument that night; between Kim and Bryna, old friends though they were.

"You want *me* to stay behind, Bryna? Well, *I won't*!"

"But Kim, you're too . . . you're too frail for such a perilous journey."

"Not too frail to stay here and be murdered in my sleep, though?"

"But you must see, you must understand . . . you would only slow us down . . . you . . . you . . ." What could Bryna say that would not simply insult the old dog?

Kim scratched his ear a moment, let Bryna stumble into silence. "Aye, well, if I am to stay behind, then maybe Sleekit should stay here with me."

"What, but—?"

Kim stood up, lifted his head proudly and began to walk slowly around the outside of their circle. "Yes, maybe I am too old, too decrepit . . . But isn't Sleekit too ill? And Saal, a barely-weaned pup, too young? Treacle and Lugger too far away from their last square meal?" He gave Bryna an odd sideways glance, too shrewd to be an accident. She did not see it, but she sensed his meaning all the same. And next to her dead Grundle was purring gently to himself.

How was any choice to be made? From the angry, reluctant wild cats to the weakest of kits. It was all, or none. All – or they were just as bad as the squabbling gangs that menaced the town.

And if the river waters never rose again? Well, then they would simply die in the wilderness. But at least they would die together.

Almost unseen, Ki-ya and Dart slunk back into the circle.

And in the end, so it was; and the remaining members of the Council prepared themselves for their journey.

Four

The Fox Again

Skrinkle-the-fox, well fed and dozy with it, lay at the entrance to his earth den.

He *should* have been happy, he *should* have been content.

Close by, his vixen, Slivid, watched with pleasure as their three small cubs fed greedily upon the body of some small animal. They did not need its meat; ate only because it was there to eat. The worst of the drought had done these foxes little harm. For them there was always water to be found, always food enough to share; and then some.

So, the fox should have been happy, he should have been content. But he was not.

How could he be happy to lie among the

dirt of a wretched wilderness when he held between his paws a power that was so great, so awesome it was almost beyond imagining? How could he be content to play happy families when he – a simple fox born – had flown upon the wind, had swum the depths of a river, climbed trees, scaled mountains, shifted the very rocks of the earth? *Could even men do better?*

Ah yes . . . men. Men, with their great, bustling towns and cities. He had studied them well. And inside his breast a deep, black jealousy burned again.

There had been one town in particular. That it now stood empty of men had surprised him at first. But then again, if men did not want it, if they had abandoned it to their silly pets, why should he not have it? Because he could! And surely, it was the least he deserved?

Forgive him for this if you can. Do not judge him too harshly for that strange twist of nature that made Skrinkle what he was. He was a throwback to a darker age, to a time when creatures of spirit and creatures of body were not so easily divided.

And how so? Do not ask. It was a thing beyond his understanding; his, yours, or mine. But he remembered vividly the first time the power had come to him. Hadn't he been just a young cub, then? A young cub separated from his kin? Hadn't men been chasing him? Vile, angry men, with their cruel foxhounds: full of hate, full of murder.

Running. Running. Running. Dogs baying wildly for his blood. The stench of death upon their foul breath. And then in panic, desperate and confused, hadn't he run in among a wood? There, by chance, glimpsed a small grey squirrel looking down upon him from the tallest branches of a tree. How curious, how calm, how distant and safe the tiny animal had looked. If only he. If only he—

Suddenly, he had felt himself climbing. Grasping leaves and branches, using limbs and nimble claws that surely weren't his own. Up he went. Up and up. And bamboozled, the stupid foxhounds at his tail had tried to follow, had stood at the bottom of the tree and bayed. Yowled in puzzlement until their angry huntsmen found them there, cursed them for fools and dragged them away by the scruff of the neck.

Unpractised and frightened, Skrinkle had held the shape of the squirrel too long; and when at last he had released himself to his own body again he was left senseless and exhausted and simply fell out of the tree. An easy victim, should the foxhounds have returned. Luckily they had not.

From that moment on he had practised his new-found skill as often as he dared. He grazed the open fields as a dull-brained bull. He slithered upon his belly as a snake. Barked as a dog. Mewed as a cat. Roared out loud as a huge brown bear. And – joy of all joys – flew the spring skies as a great hunting bird. Each time he held his adopted shape for only a short while, and yet each time it sapped his strength to exhaustion. Though it did not stop his experiments. Once, stupidly, he tried to become a man. But men's bodies, men's minds were far too complicated for him to master. The exertion almost killed him.

Slowly, painfully, he taught himself the limits of his power. He refined his skills. Learned not to bite off more than he could swallow. Kept to the animal forms he could master and to tasks easily performed. With practice he found he could move between one shape and another without first returning to his own body. It was a game he learned to play well, and a game it stayed. Until the coming of the drought.

Ah yes, the drought . . . At last he came to understand the full worth of his talents.

While all around him animals grew wasted and thin, starved and died, how well Skrinkle-the-fox ate! How varied was his diet. He grew stronger, fitter, more healthy than ever. You see, to feed the bellies of the creatures he became was to feed his own belly.

The few foxes that survived the drought, though loners by nature, gathered themselves about him. Offered themselves up to him in exchange for the eatings of a meal. And he had fed and watered them all. How often the bird had flown then: bringing fresh meat upon the talon; or leading his kin the distance to a drink. How easily was loyalty bought.

It was then that he had taken himself a mate. Slivid, the strongest, most intelligent of the surviving females. And already she had borne him cubs.

Ah ... but enough of the past, of yesterdays. *Now* was the time for greater things. *Now* Skrinkle-the-fox remembered that empty town and would have it for himself. He would have it because – because it had belonged to men. He would have it because he *could* have it. And he knew how he would go about getting it. He'd seen the dogs and cats fighting in the streets. Among all the buildings of the town he'd seen the church tower standing bold and proud of all the rest. Oh yes, he knew exactly how he would go about getting it . . .

Five

THE OUTLANDS

The ten remaining dogs and cats of the Council spent their last night in the town out in the open, upon the Town Moor. In truth there were no preparations to be made for their wild adventure. There was no hearty meal to set them on their way. Only a night's rest. Only courage to be found. They slept uneasily together, and set out at first light.

As the sun began to show above the rooftops of the town, a thin string of animals could be seen twisting its way off the Town Moor, heading towards the riverside.

Strangely enough, as they made their way

down through the streets the travellers met no opposition. No gangs, no wild dog packs trying to bar their way, or demanding bribes for safe passage. When they reached the river they even found themselves free to take a drink without the threat of an ugly fight. Word of their proposed adventure into the Outlands had spread like wildfire during the night. It was almost as if they were deliberately being allowed to pass; and if they were watched at all, they were watched in secret and at a distance. It wasn't their strength of numbers that kept the curious at bay, but something else. A fear of catching their madness? Aye, perhaps: a madness that had obviously struck them all, had them walking eagerly out of the town and towards a certain death.

As they began to follow the course of the river, Bryna's heart lightened. Dead Grundle, who had left her during the night, was once more walking quietly at her side with his small bird perched happily on his shoulder. There was a general air of feverish excitement about their whole party. So much so that, even with near-empty bellies and precious little sleep, they could not help yelping and snittering like silly pups or kits. Ki-ya and Dart encouraged them all with tales of ancient battles fought and won, of feasts and merrymaking. While Treacle and Lugger, helped where necessary by Kim, teased them with the gory stories of vicious men, and their hideous, disgusting habits.

Just as Sleekit had warned, the slight trickle of river water rose and fell at intervals: water giving way to patches of mud, giving way to long stretches of naked, dried-out river-bed, and then back to mud, then water again in turn. Until finally, the river ran dry and stayed that way.

Bryna tried to make a joke of it, said it gave them an easier road to travel. But before long the mood among them changed. One by one they all fell sullenly silent. Tails dropped between legs. And their pace, which had been slow but steady, became uncertain, hesitant and creeping. Only blind Bryna and her ghost seemed untouched, though she did sense the brooding uneasiness that had settled upon her companions. In fact their feeling went far deeper than uneasiness. It was more a kind of hopeless, heartfelt loneliness . . . an absolute, bottomless pit of loneliness.

It wasn't the loss of the water that struck them so; that had been expected. No. What had happened was simply this: they had moved beyond the outskirts of the town. Left behind them the buildings that had always stood guard over them, sheltered them, protected them even. Left behind the safety of familiar territories: well trodden prowls, snug dens, everything they knew and understood. And the farther they travelled, the farther away from that safety they went, and the deeper into an empty, endless unknown.

In truth, and to an honest eye, it was perfectly ordinary countryside that surrounded them now. The Outlands? Just trees, if wretched and leafless. Just dead grass and open fields, hedgerows and wooden fences. Just the broad, empty, dust-blown river leading forever onwards.

And Outlanders? If there were any such things, they were well hidden from the animals' eyes. Not a hide or hair, not skin or bone.

Nothing unusual then; except perhaps for the size of it all. To simple town cats and dogs used to a Town Moor neatly ringed by buildings, used to narrow streets, brick walls and close horizons, it was a vast landscape, devastatingly immense. And it seemed to swallow them up as they moved through it. Every step began to weigh more heavily upon them, every breath became more difficult to draw. Heads began to turn, to look back the way they had come. Surely, better the devil they knew than this . . .

"This is ridiculous, Bryna," hissed Treacle.

"Ridiculous, Captain," repeated Lugger.

"We'll never get anywhere at this rate. Might as well give up and go home."

"Give up and go home, Captain," repeated Lugger, with the hint of a question in his voice.

"This silly adventure wasn't my idea," spat Bryna, flicking her tail in annoyance. (Beside her, dead Grundle said nothing.)

"Nor was it mine," said Kim, who was following Bryna in line and already panting for breath.

Out in front, leading the way, Sleekit deliberately lengthened his stride, determined to press on . . .

* * *

For a long, long time the Outlands around them never changed. The dried-up river-bed simply went forever onwards; no rising water, no patch of mud. It sometimes grew broader, sometimes narrower, and its banks steeper or shallower, but it went forever onwards. And as the day warmed, the stark empty blue sky and the white horizon of the sun-bleached hilltops mingled together in a tumbling heat haze; blurring their path into endlessness.

On and on. On and on . . .

And then, quite unexpectedly, Sleekit suddenly stood still. He lifted his ears, turned his head on to one side as if he was listening for something.

"What?" cried Cherry, excitedly. "What is it?"

"Shush — Shush now. Don't you hear it? Don't any of you hear it?" said Sleekit. "And the river-bed – see how it darkens."

By now his companions had drawn level

with him, were cocking their ears, pawing the dry earth.

"I can't see anything," said Kim. "Can't hear anything either!"

"Me neither," said Ki-ya.

"Pah!" spat Dart. "And the dry earth is just the dry earth! So much for following silly kits into the middle of nowhere!"

"No! You're just not looking properly. Not listening—" Sleekit scrambled across the river-bed and between a shallow, crumbling gap in the riverbank. Once upon a time, it might well have been the outflow of a small stream coming off the distant hills. "From here . . . Try from here!"

"Well, I still can't hear anything," said Kim, following slowly after the kit. All around, animals were beginning to look worried. Fisher pulled Saal, her pup, close to her side.

Sleekit was becoming desperate. "Oh surely, Bryna, surely *you* can hear it?"

Blind Bryna was standing silently apart. Her

ears, sharpened by blindness, cut through the sound of squabbling cats and dogs. In her dark inside world, and encouraged now by dead Grundle, she roamed freely. Beyond the barren riverside, following the length of the dried-up stream as it reached upwards to the hilltops. And there at last, upon the summit, she heard it. Faint, distant, but clear. The cry of running water.

"Yes, Sleekit. I can hear it. I *can* hear it."

Instantly, their journey became more urgent. Sleekit led them out of the river valley and along the line of the stream, turning them away from the sunrise to face south. And always the way carried them uphill; slowly at first, but then more rapidly, more steeply. At several points, because of the strange way the hills leaned lazily against one another, shoulder to shoulder, any dog or cat who happened to turn around would have glimpsed their town, grey and forlorn, stretched out along the valley floor behind them. (Luckily no animal ever did, or else what little courage had brought them that far might well have deserted them for good.)

For a healthy animal, dog or cat, that climb would have gone almost unnoticed. But these adventurers were anything but healthy. Each step weighed more heavily on them than the last, only the tantalising sound of running water, real or imaginary, kept them moving at all.

"I still can't hear anything," cried Cherry in desperation.

"Well, I *think* I can hear it," said Kim, "But I'm damned if I can see it!"

"Not far now," said Sleekit, more hopeful than truthful. "Just over this hill."

"Oh, is that all, *just* over the hill," said Dart, sarcastically.

A long way off, the ridge of the hill towered over them: a solid, dark silhouette set against the brash blue sky. Oddly, the closer they came to it, the more it seemed to melt away from them. Until, as they reached the point where they were certain they should be standing on its summit, the ridge disappeared altogether; and a new ridge grew up, as far away as ever.

In this way, and still following the dry bed of the stream, they climbed endless ridge after endless ridge. Until, finally – amid a great deal of complaining, puffing and blowing – the steep slope grew less steep, and the ridge broadened out into a smooth, gently rounded summit. Cats began to cry with relief and dogs barked, as their way became easier and the sound of running water more clear.

But then, quite suddenly, something new loomed across the horizon, barred their way as surely as if the hill had reared up against them.

Whatever it was, it was still some way

off, and although Bryna did not see it, she immediately sensed its immense size; the weight of it filled her head, worried her fur.

Instinctively, and almost as one body, they stopped and crouched down low, just as if they were hiding from the threat of some strange predator. Only Sleekit kept to his feet, kept moving, bewildered by the reaction of his companions. "What is the matter? Do you think it's going to bite? It's a fence! Only a fence! And our drink of water is on the other side of it."

In truth, it was a fence. A giant of a metal fence; man-made, and stretching out endlessly across the skyline. There wasn't a twist or a turn in it, not a beginning nor an end: and only changing its shape where, every so often, an even taller giant – a huge metal tower – grew up out of it.

And water? Ah yes, there was water. Lying

on the ground some distance behind the fence but still following the line of the hills, a strange almost animal-like pipe wriggled and snaked. The pipe-creature was obviously badly injured because in more than one place thin bursts of water exploded from its body, gathering together in shallow puddles that reached out towards the fence. And the wounds were not new; the edges of the puddles were stained green where new shoots of grass had found the strength to grow.

But there was something else to worry about now, something else to unnerve them all: suddenly the fence was not silent. It began to sing to them above the sound of the water. Humming sadly, one long low continuous note. A warning note.

"Oh, come on," cried Sleekit. "What do you want us to do, turn back? Give up, after we've come so far? Well I for one won't! And look, *look*! There's even a dog-sized hole in the fence to crawl through. It might have been made for us coming!"

Slowly at first, and overcome with curiosity, dizzy with thirst, dogs and cats began to pluck up the courage to move cautiously towards the singing fence.

"After all, like he says, it's only a fence, Bryna," said Treacle, trying to put a brave face on it.

"Only a fence, Captain," echoed Lugger.

"Yes, but why does it sing to us, then?" asked Fisher, using the weight of her paws to hold down her excited pup.

"Oh, that'll be the wind running through its wires, that's all," said Cherry.

"It doesn't *sound* like the wind—" said Bryna cautiously, but brave enough to feel her way forwards.

And then, unexpected, there was Grundle, no longer walking passively at her side, but standing in her way. His teeth bared, his open claws raised, as big and brutal as ever they had been in life. Inside her head dark shadows fell. Had he turned against her? Then she heard his stark warning—

"Stay, Bryna. Stay, pussy! There is only death here—!"

In that same instant, in a wild flurry of feathers, the sparrow upon Grundle's back rose up into the air, as if it, on its own, could block Bryna's way. But already the time for phantoms was passed. The ghost cat was gone and the bird with it.

The day felt suddenly cold even beneath the burning heat of the sun, and the doleful singing of the fence seemed to close in upon Bryna.

All around her there was confusion. Cats and dogs moving excitedly towards the wire fence. Ki-ya and Dart, even Kim among them. Bryna tried to make her own warning. Opened her throat, caterwauled. "Listen to the song of the wire," she cried out. "Heed its warning!"

No animal was listening. There were only excited laughs in return.

Unseen by Bryna, it was Cherry the greyhound who made it first to the fence – before Sleekit, even – and with Treacle and Lugger already at her tail. The dog lowered her head and began to twist her body through the small hole there.

"Come on, follow me! I'm as good as through already! Can't you almost taste that water? It's easy, see—?"

The singing wire stopped singing and shrieked at them. The whole sky came suddenly alive, flashed and snapped with the brilliance of a second sun, vibrating with a livid colour as the cry grew louder.

The poor dog beneath the fence fell instantly dead. Bryna sensed the killing made. But the cruel tragedy unfolding around her did not end there. Again and again thc wires cried out in wild frenzy; burned flesh soured the air with its stench. And the longer the wire raged the further its unseen jaws stretched out among them.

Snap snap. Snap snap.

"Run — Quickly, run," Bryna heard Treacle's final cry and Lugger's feeble response.

"Run, Captain—" She heard no more from either; could only imagine their poor bodies caught beneath the fence.

Bryna bared *her* teeth then, opened *her* claws. Her first instinct was to attack the strange enemy; but somehow she knew she must not. She held herself fast, called out in bitter anguish at the loss of her friends. This was no enemy a cat or a dog could hope to fight . . .

No animal moved now; not towards the singing fence, not away from it. They huddled close together against the ground, stricken, like things of stone. The touch of their bodies their only comfort, their only hold on reality.

Slowly, Bryna felt her senses returning . . . First, came the distinct sound of animals breathing heavily. Then the smell of fright, the smell of the dry, sun-scorched earth beneath her paws.

And then she heard the humming noise.

The wire fence was singing a new, sad, mournful note.

Bryna's ears pricked as the crying note of the wire seemed to change a second time. Not a call of sadness now, but not a squall of anger either. More a gentle, distant throbbing. She stood up, pulled herself out of the slight hollow she found herself in, wanted to get a better sense of what was happening. And all around dogs and cats followed her.

The constant low hum of the wire *still* sounded. This new noise wasn't a changed note at all – it was a *second* note. A second noise coming from somewhere behind the fence, and getting louder, getting closer.

"Bryna? Bryna, what is it?" cried Sleekit. "There's *something* out there on the hillside. Something moving this way."

Bryna felt her heart race. Some of the animals there were too young to remember, but surely they had not *all* forgotten *that* sound? Not Ki-ya or Dart, not Kim—?

Well, Bryna remembered it well enough: the crunch and grind of an engine's gear box. The roar of a metal road machine.

Already the stench of its exhaust fumes, the pungent taste of its oil and its burning petrol was filling her head. Could it be true?

The roaring became louder still as the huge metal animal charged along the line of the hill towards them.

And then, above everything else, came the smell of living men. There was no mistaking that. The slightly stale, sweet odour; the sickly mixture of natural body smells and those other peculiar, man-made scents that curdled together into one.

How many times since man's disappearance from the town had Bryna pictured this moment of reunion? Running happily to greet Mrs Ida Tupps. (She had no reason to believe any other person would come seeking her out.) The joy. The overwhelming sense of relief. The feeling of safety.

But Bryna did not move, could not move, not to run and greet them, not to turn and run away. Suddenly she was paralysed (and her companions were paralysed with her). There was no feeling of joy. Only . . . only what? Was it fear? Yes. But then again not a fear she readily understood. A mixture of dread and loathing. Not hatred exactly, but she knew she did not want these men near her, whoever they were. She did not want them near her. She did not want their help. She did not want them there at all.

The lap-cat, the common house-pet she had once been, was gone. Long gone.

The great metal beast growled louder,

before it came to a sudden halt behind the wire fence and the cry of its engine died in its metal throat. There was more clanking and clicking as heavy metal doors were swung open, as heavy-booted feet stamped their way down metal footplates and on to the ground. The feet shuffled their way towards the break in the wire.

Then . . . voices.

Six

THE GREEN METAL MEN

"What the heck's been goin' on here? Look at that ruddy hole in the fence, will you?" More shuffling feet. "I *told* you there were flamin' animals."

"What d'you mean, *told* us?"

"I told you! Said I could see them from the watch tower. And there you are, Jock. Look – animals! Cats and ruddy dogs."

"You must have a bloody good pair of eyes on you, that's all I can say!"

"Never heard of binoculars, Jock?"

"Aye, well, you're supposed to be a border guard. You're supposed to be looking out for that old town from the tower, not eyeing up the wild life, Smithie. Anyway,

I can see them now: and what a stink! Their skin's been burnt to a ruddy crisp on them wires."

"Don't get yourself too close or you'll be joinin' them," said a third voice. "That border fence is electrified and it's still live, remember."

The man called Smithie knelt down carefully and began picking at the bodies, through the hole in the fence, with a long wooden stick. "Here, this one's wearing a flippin' collar, Coots."

"Never."

"It is. 'Am telling you – a collar."

"There's nobody living out this close to the border; not with pets. Not any more," said Jock.

"You don't suppose they're left over from the evacuation, do you?" said Coots.

"Nah, not after all this time—"

"Heh up, Jock. Will you look at this though?" interrupted Smithie, suddenly excited. "There's a couple of the little beggars still breathing."

"Yer what, Smithie?"

"Still alive, I'm telling you. That big brown tatty-rag of a cat, and his little mate there next to him."

"Aye, well, you'd best put them out of their misery. I mean, they've just had ten thousand volts shoved up their backsides."

Smithie used his stick as a lever to turn them over, to get a proper look at them. First Treacle and then Lugger. Satisfied, he slowly stretched out an arm, and one at a time, gently scooped them up in his huge hand, pulled them back through the hole in the fence and pushed them inside his open tunic."

"Yer soft old beggar," Coots laughed. "What are you goin' to do with them? They're already half-cooked."

"That's it, isn't it, Smithie? A nice tasty little cat casserole—" mocked Jock. "Anything's got to be better than the rubbish they've been forcing us to swallow since rationing started." They all laughed.

"And anyway, Smithie, you know the rules. Nowt's supposed to come over that fence, dead or alive: not man or beast. They've probably got themselves a dose of sommat. Sommat catching, an' all."

"Oh, bog off you two, will you?" said Smithie. "You've got no soul."

"Well, just keep the little beggars well away from me, that's all I'm saying. Keep them away from me: or else I'll give their little necks an extra twist for 'em."

"You're all heart, Jock. All heart . . ."

"Aye, well, never mind all that, you've saved yourself them, but what are you goin' to do about the rest?"

"The rest?"

"Aye, out there, t'other side of the wire. In the middle of the field. There's a whole bunch of live 'uns; just sitting there staring at us. Creepy so-and-sos. The place is bloody well infested with animals."

Blind though she was, Bryna sensed that they'd been seen. But still she could not bring herself to move. She sat transfixed, listening to their prattle; it had been so long since she'd heard men's voices she didn't really understand their words. Only knew they'd taken poor Treacle's body.

Closest to her was Fisher, with Saal tucked in hard against her flanks, watching the men intently. The men were standing on the far side of the fence, in a small huddle around the hole. The pup had never seen men before. But they were nothing like he'd imagined them to be, not after all the strange tales he'd been told. For one thing these men all looked exactly the same: they were green from head to foot! For another they were only half as tall as he expected them to be. And they didn't seem to be very special in any way . . .

if anything, they were rather comical. On top of their heads they were all wearing strange metal hats that were as big as iron buckets and had odd bits of twig and broken branches sticking out of them. And in their arms they all carried identical, long metal sticks.

"What are they doing?" asked Bryna. "I can hear their words, but I can't see them."

"I don't know. I've never seen anything like it. They look so funny," said Fisher. "Two of them are pointing at us with their metal sticks."

"Bryna, *I* don't like it," Saal whined. "Tell them to stop, they're making me scared."

Something made the animals run then. All of them, without the need to be told – each bolting instinctively in a different direction, as if they understood they had to spread the target. Afterwards, Bryna swore dead Grundle had come to her again, had bullied her out of her stupor and pushed her off across the hillside. Maybe he did. Maybe it was a deeper instinct.

Rack rack! Rack rack!

In the same instant that the noise of gunfire cut the air, the solid ground beneath their paws exploded, showered them with stinging fragments of stone and dry dirt; and something sliced the tip of Bryna's tail clean off with brutal agony.

As she ran, Bryna briefly sensed Ki-ya and Dart moving away to her left, Kim and Sleekit to her right. Deliberately, she threw herself down the slope of the hill, away from them. It was every animal for themselves. They must each make their escape as best they could, and she did not want to draw the gunfire down upon her friends.

Rack rack! Rack rack!

The men, the soldiers – because, of course, soldiers is what they were – began laughing again. And luckily, they were being lazy, not bothering too much about finding their targets. On a whim they turned their sights across the length of the hill. Their second rounds buried deep in the ground close behind Kim and Sleekit, but without harming them.

"How'd you manage to miss from this range, eh, Jock?"

"I didn't miss, Coots old son. Got myself one of 'em at least!"

"Oh, yeah, and I suppose pigs can fly, can they? How come I just saw *your* targets scampering off down the hill, then?"

Suddenly there was a new voice coming from inside the truck, shouting angrily against the burst of gunfire. "Hoi, you lot, what the bloody hell do you think you're doing? Starting world war bloody three?"

"Awe, it's just a bunch of strays, Sarge."

"Aye, if we don't finish them off now they'll only be back again messing with the fence. They're all half-starved anyway. We're doing them a favour."

"I'll do you a bloody favour in a minute. Try using your imagination, will you? You're on active service now, not playing toy soldiers; supposed to be guarding your country's border! Firing live rounds across a neutral zone! Breaking every rule in the book! And what would you do if the other side decided to fire back at you?"

"Now who's using his imagination, Sarge? There's five miles between our fence and theirs. An' sweet all in the middle for us to worry about; 'cept empty countryside and ghost towns. I couldn't even see them if I were standing at the top of me watch tower, with a pair of Smithie's binoculars in me hand—"

"Don't get smart with me, son. Right, Jock, you seem to have started all this, you can have the privilege of guarding the hole in the fencc until the lick and stick mob get here to fix it. And see if you can't get them to plug up them damned leaks in that plastic water pipe. There's little enough of the stuff to go around as it is, without watering the daisies. The rest of you – back in the truck."

"Awe, where's your sense of fun, Sarge? There's only a few of 'em out there—"

"In the truck. Now!"

Seven

From Bad to Worse

With the echo of gunfire ringing in his ears, Kim had run away from the wire fence and the green metal men. He had run away, and had kept on running. Abandoning all. Hurling himself across the hillside like a dog gone mad. Travelling too fast and too far for his decrepit old body. Only stopped when his legs finally gave way beneath him and refused to be picked up again; forcing him to rest, sprawled clumsily in the dirt where he fell.

"You're a bloody daft old beggar, Kim. Ayc, a bloody daft old beggar," he swore to himself between short gasping breaths.

The whole silly adventure had been an

awful mistake, a mockery from the very start. Leaving the protection of the town! He should have seen the stupidity of it. They had been beaten at their very first fence! *And* by men! . . . *Men!* That name no longer set his heart pounding or his tail beating as it once might have done. In fact, the very thought of men turned his stomach, or at least, filled him up with wind.

It was only then, as he lay listening to his own desperate breath, that he heard the kicking wheeze of some other animal's breath . . . That poor diseased excuse for a cat, Sleekit: there was no mistaking him. Every step Kim had taken, Sleekit had followed. When he had run, the kit had run. When he had stumbled, the kit had stumbled with him.

"Well, Sleekit, where is your brotherhood now—? Running scared across a barren hillside? That, or lying somewhere dead . . . ?"

"Can any of us be blamed for trying?" said Sleekit, breathless.

Could they?

Kim gave up on the argument. In truth, he was fond of the sickly kit, and maybe he was too old to remember the blind optimism of youth.

They did not stay in that exposed place for long. Once they had caught their breath and gathered their senses, they began, in their feeble-bodied way, to search for their lost friends. Slowly, cautiously, they worked their way across the hillside, back towards the wire fence, only to find it still well-guarded and no sign of other animals. They tried moving away from it, only to find themselves moving in vague circles, drawn back there again and again, like moths to a flame. Unwilling to give up.

On their last approach, their hearts leapt. No soldiers, no green metal men. And sitting close to the fence, as bold as brass, were

Ki-ya and Dart, Fisher and Saal. And if they all looked the worse for wear, at least they were alive.

"The men are gone," announced Ki-ya, matter-of-factly, "gone, and taken the hole in the fence with them. Taken the water too—"

Impossible though it seemed, it was true. New wire hastily criss-crossed the old, filling in the hole; and the fence was proudly singing a new note, as if to show off its repair. And behind the fence? No excitable trickle of water called out to them, enticing them to try their luck with the singing wire. The pipe-creature lay silent and still, its seeping wounds bound tight with tape and gauze, though they could make no sense of it.

Those foolish cats and dogs waited by that fence far longer than was safe, hoping against hope that, just as they had been drawn back there, so, too, blind Bryna would return.

It fell dark, came light again, before they crept away for the last time . . .

Even then, they were unwilling to give up completely on the blind cat: they ran wild upon the lowland hills for almost two days. Two cruel days; two desperate nights. Long tortured by an unforgiving drought, the Outlands gave them almost nothing. Not one single sign of Bryna; not hair or breath. And little to eat. Less to drink.

Dart found them the carcass of a wood pigeon that had fallen unnoticed from the sky and been caught, spread-eagled, among the bare branches of a dead tree. And once they even cornered and killed a rat between them. But neither bird nor rodent were worth the bother of eating.

There was a simple truth: the exposed hillside, the gaping, endless wilderness that was the Outlands was not a natural part of their world. Not even for Ki-ya, Dart or

Sleekit, all long used to the open spaces of their beloved Town Moor. So far away from their own territory, they felt defenceless, naked and exposed beyond all reason. And as if to prove the point, at almost every turn they took they glimpsed a view of a deep river valley and a town – their town – standing distant and grey, but more solid somehow, more real than that awful dust-blown wilderness they now stood upon. And with the heat of the day, the warm motions of air rising up from its streets, it seemed almost to be beckoning to them, calling them back.

And in the end so it was, starved for the lack of food, befuddled for the lack of water, they forgot about blind Bryna. They turned their heads once more towards the town, and began to make their long way home; or else they would all have surely died there . . .

Eight

Treacle in the Dark

As Kim led the few remaining members of the Council down off the Outland hills, in some other distant place Treacle was waking up in the dark.

It was a strange, lingering dark that was not complete black. He could not say where he was, or how he had come to be there. His sleep had been long, deep and empty; without thought or feeling. Only when at last he opened his eyes was there the pain of hurt. A far-off, numbing hurt that seemed to linger in his bones.

Then, to his surprise, he discovered Lugger lying there next to him. His friend was breathing low and evenly in a restful sleep, not yet disturbed by the agony of wakefulness.

At last Treacle began to remember . . . The battle with the singing wires; the dreadful power of its sting. Then the vague idea that there had been men arguing, that he had been lifted up off the ground and carried . . .

Soon, Lugger too was awake.

They had been placed together inside some kind of box. A small slatted wooden crate that let the air in and allowed them to breathe. There was a hinged lid, but it could not be opened from the inside; no matter how much they bit and clawed at it.

Mostly they were left to themselves. Caged in. With no room to move about or even to stretch out properly; nowhere to relieve their bowels in private.

Sometimes though, just sometimes, a door would open close by, squeaking on its hinges.

And for an instant a sharp prick of daylight would leap across the floor and flick through the slats in the side of their box. Then would come the footsteps, the heavy breathing of men, and their constant, cold-mouthed jibber-jabber. Usually, in a few short moments the door would clang shut again, taking the men with it. But other times, when the door clanged shut, the men did not go away. There would be different kinds of voices; soft, eager, whispered voices. The lid of their box would be lifted up. And then would come the man-handling, the strange touches, the back-tingling strokes. Treacle wanted to hiss and spit, to rake the stroking hands with his open claws and draw blood. But the voices were so gentle, so seductive, he could not stop the purr from rising up in his throat to greet them.

"There, there, bonnie lad, don't fret so . . . Got you some decent grub for a change."

"You've gone soft in the head, Smithie.

You think more of them bloody cats than you do of your own children."

"Naff off, Jock."

"What you going to do with them then? Fatten them up for Christmas? Send them home in a food parcel?"

"Naff off!" Smithie scooped up Treacle and Lugger, cradled them in his arms together, like tiny babies.

"Well, you can't keep them in this store-room forever, can you? 'Should have wrung their ruddy necks, left them at the border fence, like I said. Sarge is goin' to cotton on sometime."

"Listen – like I said, just naff off, before I stick my boot where the sun don't shine."

"All right, all right, Smithie. Keep your hair on," laughed Jock. "I'm going, I'm going . . ."

Afterwards, when Treacle and Lugger were dropped back into the box, when the lid was closed and the stroking hands were gone, there was always food and water waiting for them. Not scraps either, or rotting rancid lumps of carrion that stank of stale blood, but warm sweet-tasting meats. Treacle had been a young kit the last time he had tasted the foods of men; he had almost forgotten their delights.

And so, Treacle and Lugger survived in captivity. More than that, they thrived in their small dark prison. They took the food and the drink. They took the fondling hands, the stroking and the petting, the silly baby talk. Took it as the price they had to pay for their lives.

And they detested it. Detested everything about it. Waited for a chance to make their escape, to make their bid for freedom.

"One day, Lugger," promised Treacle.

"One day, Captain," echoed Lugger.

It was to be a long wait . . .

Nine

A Gruesome Hoard

Skrinkle-the-bird had found himself the perfect rooftop perch; the bell-tower of a tall red-bricked church. The church had been built only halfway up the valley side, but by chance stood upon a stone outcrop that set it clear of all the buildings, the ugly mishmash of warehouses, factories and department stores that now surrounded it. The view it gave him was spectacular.

It was very early, the last of the stars still pricked the morning sky. All around him the town lay solemn and grey. Its empty buildings seemed to stand too heavily upon their foundations; as if they had grown weary of the constant beating of the sun, but were steeling themselves for its imminent return. The few solitary four-footers who moved about the streets looked his way passively, if they looked at all. Obviously they did not know him yet, or they would not have walked so boldly.

They would all know him soon enough. Skrinkle had prepared his coming well.

Time and again he had become Skrinkle-the-bird and flown unnoticed into the town. He knew by heart the ways of its streets as they criss-crossed the valley sides. He understood the strange coursing of the river water as it struggled to cut its way across the dried-up valley floor. More importantly, he had studied the dogs and the cats. They were so great in number and yet so weak and feeble; always squabbling, fighting among themselves. No trust. No brotherhood. Easy meat for such as himself . . .

And now he had come to the town for good.

The weight of the bird's body began to hang heavily upon him: he had worked long and hard that night and he was weary of it. All around and about him in that tower lay the reminder of his labours. The carcasses of animals and birds gathered from far and wide. Rat and vole. Squirrel and lamb. Goat and hen, magpie and pigeon; and more. It was a gruesome hoard, and yet no less wondrous for that.

At the centre of the bell-tower there was a broad open shaft, a hole big enough to give him easy access to the inside of the church. He began to use his wings to guide himself into the shaft, and as he did he heard his mate, Slivid, far below, calling out to him from where she lay with their cubs in the dark.

"Skrinkle? Skrinkle is that you? Is it done—? Are we set—?" All around her other foxes began to stir.

"So many questions! So much noise! Do

you want to scare the poor doggies in the street? . . . Aye. Aye, it's done. And well done, too. Now, let me rest!"

At that the bird was gone and there was only the fox. He fell heavily against his mate, exhausted with the night's efforts.

Ten

Homecoming

It was broad daylight. The sun already burning hot. Kim sat looking sadly down upon the stark, shadow-filled streets of the town. He had not expected to see them again. His body shook in fevered spasms, its strength all but gone. And his mind, befuddled for the lack of a drink, tried to make sense of it all. He thought for a moment about blind Bryna, and the humming wire, about stinging gunfire . . . and the dead.

"Well, Kim, we have come back. What do we do now?" asked Ki-ya.

"*Do*?" It was Sleekit who answered. "Survive, if we can . . . Just survive."

"Go your own way, Ki-ya. Make the best

of it while there's still some life in you," said Kim, morosely. "My friends, where's the sense in *any* of you staying with me . . . waiting to see an old dog die?"

Saal began to whine, and backed nervously against his mother.

Sleekit, standing at Kim's side, licked feebly at the diseased wounds that covered his body and left his fur a tat of patches. A soft, gentle purr rose up in his throat. He had grown attached to the old mongrel, wished he could have known him in his prime. They had all come a very long way together; none of them were about to strike out on their own, even supposing they had the will or the strength to do it.

"Oh, you've been dying for more seasons than I've been alive," said Sleekit. He looked at Kim thoughtfully. "You'll see me out . . ."

Kim struggled to stand up. "Aye. Aye, well . . . Perhaps we should go out on to the streets one more time. Plead with the gangs. Make the bloody fools see the sense in sharing what little there's left here."

His companions said nothing. Ki-ya only shook his head sadly, knew that it was a hopeless task. And a mad task, too? Probably. Knew that they would try anyway . . .

Kim led the way as they began to prowl the outskirts of the town together. In truth, he did not expect to get very far without being challenged by some pack of animals or other, some desperate gang; but he stubbornly refused to keep to the little-used back lanes just to avoid a confrontation. What the heck—! What was the worst that could happen? They could only get themselves killed; and what with the wretched state they were all in, there were worse ways to die than in a clean fight.

Kim's raised spirits didn't stop him from being careful. He held back, steadied himself at every street corner, and took a long deep breath before deciding which way to turn.

Strangely, each new street stood as empty as the one before it. On the outskirts that did not surprise him, but the farther into the town they walked, the more the emptiness began to worry him. He kept on moving, and luckily the others followed on without protest.

At the next corner, another deep breath.

Another empty street.

By now they were deep within the town, but there still wasn't an animal, a dog or a cat, to be seen. No sight, no sound, no smell. Not even a lone bird crying against the heat of the sun.

"Where've they all got to?" hissed Sleekit.

"I *don't* like this," said Dart. "I don't like any of this. I wish we had Bryna's nose to help us."

"Shush," commanded Ki-ya. "Listen—"

"What for? There isn't anything to hear," said Dart.

"Yes there is, sister. Far away. In the distance . . ."

"Oh yes, *yes* . . . But that sounds just like . . . running water. And a – a big water. Like a river!"

"Like a river," repeated Kim, not quite believing it.

"But how? *How*?" cried Sleekit. "There isn't enough water in the river to raise a ripple, let alone to make that sort of noise. Hasn't been since the last rain fell." Sleekit looked up at the sky, half-expecting to see the heavy grey weight of a thunderstorm. The sky was an endless, empty, monotonous blue. He listened again.

"I can *still* hear the river . . ."

"But you can't have a river without water to feed it!" said Fisher. "It doesn't make sense."

Maybe they had all caught drought madness? Maybe they were still lost upon the Outland hills and did not know it? Maybe they were hearing things, and it was only the watery cry of the pipe-creature behind the wire fence calling to them, while death closed in all around?

Then came the other noises. Sounds that got themselves mixed up with the running water: sounds like dogs barking excitedly, and cats wailing. And not the angry noises of animals fighting either. More like . . . like animals *playing* together, crying with pleasure.

The town was real enough. Kim picked up his pace, as best he could, and in desperation began leading them towards the riverside.

What did they expect to find there? The old town bridge was a ruin; its stones stood up like a row of cracked teeth between the dried-up riverbanks. At best the only sign of the river would be a feeble, broken ribbon of water winding its way apologetically between the stones; all but lost in the immensity of the desolation.

That is what they *should* have found. But they didn't. Not that morning.

Somehow, several of the fallen stones from the old bridge had been moved. Impossible though it was, they had been lifted, dragged or pushed until they were locked solidly together. Until they had become a wall, blocking the river's path; stopping it in its tracks like a dam. Exactly like a dam. On one side of the wall a huge, growing pool of water had gathered. While on the other side even the thin trickle of water had disappeared altogether.

In the pool, groups of dogs were splashing wildly about, heedless of the newcomers. Cats too, silly with excitement, were jumping in and out, playing scaredy-cat with the rippling shallows. And more and more animals were arriving all the time.

"Come on in," yelped some dog, mischievously. "Have yourselves some fun! You look as if you need it!"

The dog-pup, Saal, began to whine, his tongue stinging with pain; the agony of going without a drink for so long suddenly too much for him. Fisher had to use her teeth to stop him from leaping forward. But the pup was not the only desperate fool among them—

Kim, too, almost leapt forward. *Almost.* The pool of water *was* a wonderful sight. But it was much more than that. Something awesome. In a way, terrifying. The stuff of miracles, or the ranting tales of cats and dogs gone mad. Could any animal have possibly made this thing? He lifted his nose to the air, half-expecting to find the stink of men hanging there. There was no man scent, but some other creature – some creature he did not recognise – had been there.

And what of the crowd of animals that had gathered around that pool, greedily lapping up its water? Weren't they the very same dogs and cats who, only a few days ago, would have been at each other's throats over such a prize as this? More strangely still, for each new arrival who joined the throng, one of the revellers would give way and make off along the riverside road as if they were heading for the warehouses, the abandoned shops and factories that lined the valley sides.

"What *is* going on here?" asked Sleek-it.

"There's only one way to find out," said Ki-ya. Mustering what strength he could, he deliberately stood in the way of a young kit as she pulled herself out of the pool. "My young friend, where are you all going to in such a hurry?"

"Where've *you* been hiding yourself?" The kit answered, full of careless cheek. "I'm not about to miss a meal for any animal!" She made to move around Ki-ya as if the bigger tom cat was no more than an inconvenience in her way.

"Y'what—?" hissed Ki-ya.

"There's free food to be had as well as free water, of course."

Taking Ki-ya's lead, Kim began to growl. "Talk some sense, will you?" He took hold of the kit by the scruff of the neck and dangled her off the ground.

"What is the matter with you lot? Gerroff, will you!" Worried now, the kit looked along the line of puzzled faces confronting her. "They say there's been meat, falling from the sky, as heavy as any rain!" With a scuff of her paw she managed to slip free of Kim's weakened grip and scooted off up the street before she could be caught again.

"Meat, falling like rain? What do you mean?" Kim called after her, but she was gone.

There was nothing else for it; bemused, the six companions each took their turn among the other dogs and cats, had that long-awaited drink and then followed after the kit.

Eleven

The Gorging

They did not have far to go. What they saw between the long lines of dishevelled, concrete and corrugated iron warehouses, between the elderly red-bricked factories and shops, was perhaps the strangest sight they had ever seen. Neither Kim nor Sleekit, Dart, Ki-ya nor Fisher could do more than stare in awestruck wonder. The dog-pup, Saal, hid his face in his mother's flank; in case in the looking it would all suddenly disappear.

"Mother, is it the hunger sickness? Or can there really be so much food still left in all the world?"

Torn and broken carcasses – birds and

animals, large and small – lay strewn everywhere. So great was their number it was difficult to count them apart. Their killing had been expertly, if brutally, made. Bones cleanly snapped, bodies only cut or bruised where talon or claw had been forced to make the death wound. And if much of it was old meat, near rancid and only just edible, almost as much again was fresh kill, glistening, painted bright red in its own blood.

It was as if some creature had deliberately emptied its entire larder there.

In the midst of it all, dogs and cats stanced, heads to the ground, greedily gorging themselves. Some among them, already bellyful and sated, lay flat out, carelessly basking in the sun. While kits and pups dragged headless chickens up and down the pavements in wild games of catch-me-if-you-can.

"I don't believe it," said Kim, vacantly.

But the stench of the kill was real enough; it had them all drooling at the mouth.

It was something other than disbelief that held them back, stopped them from taking their share. Suspicion? Perhaps. That, or an ingrained wariness, come about after their cruel encounters upon the Outlands. They simply had to find out what had happened there, before they gave in to the demands of ravenous hunger. Each of them tried in turn, but could get no sense out of the feeding animals; their heads were too full, too excited, too drunk with the blood scent.

And then there was a sudden commotion among the revellers that rippled through their ranks. An instant reaction to a new sound – a heavy, snap-flap-flapping – that had excited pups and kits staring up at the sky, howling and squealing in eager anticipation. "Look, look — here comes the bird. Here he comes again—!"

"Aye! And with another talon full of fresh meat, an' all!"

Kim's ears pricked as he tried to follow the noise to its source.

Sure enough, there, above them all, circling in long, slow, lazy loops, flew a bird.

Skrinkle-the-bird, though no animal there knew it.

He was a strange sight. This bird did not belong in a town. His body was too massive, the spread of his wings too wide. As he moved he seemed to cast a shadow across the whole sky. And this bird was obviously a fighter. A warrior. A hunter. A meat-eater. His broad, yellow beak curved down to a razor-like point. His heavy talons were massive and well practised; and they held within their grasp some poor prey already long since dead.

"Wouldn't it be wonderful to fly . . . to prowl across the skies like that," said Sleekit, watching the flight of the bird with undisguised admiration.

"I'd rather keep my paws firmly on the

ground, if it's all the same to you," said Kim.

There was momentary panic among feeding dogs and cats as the great warrior bird suddenly swooped low across the street. They drew back in alarm, only to lunge eagerly forwards again as he passed them by. He had deliberately dropped his latest victim among them, and he turned upon the air to watch, with obvious pleasure, as it was greedily torn apart.

Then, satisfied with himself, Skrinkle-the-bird looped one last arrogant circle across the sky. And, as cats and dogs watched, he disappeared into the dark shadows of a tall tower that seemed to swallow him whole.

"Has he flown away, again?" asked Dart.

"No—" said Ki-ya, "No. I'm sure he's gone *inside* that tower . . ."

To Kim's eyes, the tower was part of a very strange building. It stood only halfway up the valley side. But because of an odd outcrop of rock at that exact point, it seemed to stand proud and taller than *all* the buildings that surrounded it. In fact everything about that building seemed tall. Too tall. As if it had been built deliberately, impressively out of scale. The pinnacled roof and bell-tower. The dirt-marked windows that ran almost from the ground to the roof line, and yet let no light in or out again. The heavy wood and iron door at its base, and the long row of worn stone steps that ran up to it. All too tall. Above the huge door, cut deep into the weather-stained stone mantle, were the words IN GOD WE TRUST. 1917. But across the carved stone there was a second text spelled out in big brash plastic lettering, that added YATES AN– SONS MACHIN–TOOLS. Though the animals did not know it, the building was a disused church become factory, and now a disused church again.

They continued to stare up at the tower long after the bird had disappeared. And as they watched there came a new, odd mixture of sounds to their ears. First, a hacking bellow and a rumbling thud; like some giant beast was stomping about inside the church, trying to find its feet. Then, a series of deafening hollow cracks, like splintering wood, and the pop-popping of exploding metal rivets. Suddenly, the huge wood and iron door – a door that had stood stubbornly closed against dog and cat for as long as any of them could remember – burst open upon its hinges. It was an impressive sight. It was also a terrifying sight. Some animals squealed with fear, some howled with excitement, but most simply stared dumbly. Only men opened closed doors, they all knew that. If some animal was trying to make a point, it was a point well made.

The showing off wasn't done with. Out through the open doorway stepped an odd-looking dog-like animal. A female, she stood about Kim's size, but with a lithe body and a long sleek fur coat, the colour of rusted tin. Her legs looked almost too thin to support her body. While her huge bushed tail, tipped with white, seemed out of proportion to the rest of her. Her muzzle was long and thin and came almost to a point. Her eyes sparkled like small, glittery yellow-and-black buttons, and her ears sat forward upon her head; always upright and alert. Her scent was strong too, even over the smell of freshly-spilled blood: and it was strangely unsettling, bristling Kim's fur, making him feel as if he needed to wash.

This was no dog. And never a man's plaything or feral animal – no pet gone wild – but a true wild beast, born of the Outlands. A she-fox. A vixen.

Close behind the vixen followed several more of her kind. Three sets walking as pairs. While two or three lone dog-foxes stood watching discreetly from the shadows of the doorway. It struck Sleekit how very little there was to mark the foxes apart; they all looked as sharp-witted, as keenly sly as the vixen who led them.

The vixen lifted her head proudly, and began to walk slowly down the stone steps of the church with her procession following on behind. She stopped, deliberately, half-way, keeping her head well above even the biggest of the dogs that stood before her. There she waited in silence.

At last there came again the hacking bel-low and the rumbling thud from deep within the church that had animals cowering in the streets. Then, from out of the darkness, there lumbered a giant. The biggest four-legged beast any dog or cat had ever seen. It was so huge it threw a shadow all the way down the steps and out into the middle of the street. Its great bulk and broad stance told Ki-ya and Dart that it was related to the gawp-eyed bullocks that had once grazed upon the Town Moor, except this animal was twice their size. Almost as tall as the doorway it walked through, almost as wide. This was a full-grown bull.

The vixen's procession began to move forwards again.

Now Kim understood how the fallen stones of the bridge had been moved to make the dam. He also understood about the opening of the great door of the church. The bull was obviously so powerful, he could have knocked down the whole building if he'd set his mind to it.

Kim was beginning to wonder if he hadn't somehow fallen asleep and found himself in the middle of a wild mixed-up nightmare. Cats and dogs together was one thing, but surely there was something unnatural about this alliance? Warrior birds, bulls and foxes—! These creatures did not belong together.

There was something else about them too, something more sinister, more worrying. In a time of extreme drought, and the most desperate of shortages, they were *all* sleek-furred, fit, strong and healthy, without a hint of disease or illness between them.

Ki-ya and Dart looked up at the sky, both certain that the bird would reappear to complete this strange parade. But to their wonder he did not.

The vixen seemed to spot Kim then. Or did she deliberately pick him out? She stood still, cocking her head his way as if surprised, and brought her procession to a sudden, ragged stop.

"*My friend*, you do not eat? Please, take your share of meat. You and your companions here. There's plenty to go round. And plenty more where that came from. Or my name's not Slivid, nor is Skrinkle my master and my mate, and he is. He is!" She turned her eyes upon the bull, who only snorted in agreement. "Come now, we did not intend to spoil your meal with such a grand entrance. And you look as if you could do with a good feed." Slivid picked up a small, but particularly fresh and bloody haunch from among the carcasses that lay strewn about the street, and made a great show of personally dropping it between Kim's open front paws. "Go on, take a bite. It won't bite back, I promise."

"'Welcome to my parlour,' said the spider to the fly!" Dart hissed under her breath.

"Pardon?" asked Slivid.

"Why so generous a gift, *my friend*?" said Ki-ya.

The vixen stared long and hard at the three-legged tom cat and again flashed an eye towards the bull.

"Aye, tell us, what's in it for you?" spat Dart.

There were raised murmurs among the gathered cats and dogs. Ears twitched, noses lifted from the ground, suddenly curious. They were most of them bellyful and contented. Extremely contented. They did not like to see their new benefactors spoken to in such a harsh way.

"We have more than enough for ourselves. Is my master, Skrinkle, to be blamed for wanting to share it?" said Slivid with a wild flourish of her tail. "Or would you *all* rather go back to fighting among yourselves for the lickings of a soiled puddle and a mouthful of old rats' droppings?" She spoke cheerfully, modestly, politely by turns. (Far too politely, Ki-ya thought.)

More murmurs, raised voices and cat calls.

"Stuff that," growled some dog. "I for one would rather have a full belly!"

"Aye, aye—! We're for Skrinkle and for Slivid! We're for the foxes!"

By now, Kim, Sleekit, Ki-ya and Dart were standing in a defensive line, with Fisher behind them, protective of her pup.

Slivid smiled patiently, took a deep breath. "Let me speak more plainly, if I can . . . Look around you, my friends, look at the members of our gathered company. We are not natural bedfellows—"

"No. No, you're not," said Ki-ya, emphatically.

"No," repeated the vixen. "No we're . . . *not.* Desperate times need desperate measures. We must all try to live together. Or else, as certain as blood is blood, we will all surely die together. Past is the time to judge any creature by the size of its teeth or the weight of its claws, the number of its legs or the cut of its wings. All here are welcome to their share . . ."

"Aye – just as long as you're not small enough to dangle from the talons of a bird!" mocked some spaniel, suddenly brave; encouraged by the cats and dogs she saw standing up to the vixen.

"I do not see you passing up your share!" said Slivid, rounding on her with bared teeth, while the bull stomped his hooves, huffed and snorted in warning.

"Aye, aye – that's true enough! That is true enough!" came the general roar of approval for the vixen. The mocking spaniel slunk away, lost herself among the gathering.

For half a moment even Kim was convinced by the vixen. Animals *together* . . . Slivid's weak philosophy did not amount to very much. But hadn't their odd alliance managed to do in one fell swoop all the things his Council had not? Between them they had fed and watered the town, ended the futile gang wars and reunited the animals. And, more importantly, it seemed that they had done it without a single blow struck in anger.

"Pah! There's still something not right here. I can't quite put my paws on it, but there's definitely something not right," cried Dart, spitting with anger. Annoyed at the way the silly animals around her were so easily impressed with Slivid's nonsense. "And if it's your mate and master who is our great benefactor, why can't he be brave enough to come and tell us himself?"

"Aye," joined in Ki-ya, "where is this Skrinkle?"

At the back of the procession the bull gave an urgent, snorting roar. His hooves drove hard against the road, left a marked gash deep in the tarmac. Dogs and cats stanced low, certain the creature was about to make a charge.

But did they believe their eyes? Still bellowing, the huge beast suddenly turned himself around and hurled himself not at them, but up the church steps; and he disappeared back through its darkened doorway.

At once, Slivid forgot her argument, simply turned her procession around and quickly followed after him.

The dogs and cats could only stand and stare blankly in bemused silence. Until, that is, Kim's curiosity finally gave way to his craving hunger. The smell of the newly-spilled blood stung his nose; it was so sweet and overpowering. He ate like a glutton, and Fisher and Saal, Sleekit, Ki-ya and Dart – aye, even Dart – ate with him. Ate until their bellies were distended with the weight of meat. Ate until the joy of being over-full had them falling into a dozy, unguarded stupor. It took Ki-ya's and Dart's wilder instincts (and the cuff of their closed paws) to persuade their companions to stand up again and move away from the centre of the town that day . . .

Skrinkle-the-fox lay upon a cold stone floor, his body shaking in worrying, fevered spasms. Too long spent in transformation. Too long the bird. Too long the bull. And too quick, too often the change made between one and the other.

His eyes were half-open, but fixed and unfocused. He knew only that he was inside his beloved church. Somewhere around him there were tall glass windows set into walls that wanted to reach upwards forever. Windows that were thick with the dirt of endless years, confusing night and day until they could not be counted apart. The space around him was a huge dark chasm that hid within it endless rows of identical metal machines. Oil-stained and angry-looking devices that had gone long unused, and were beyond the power of any poor animal to understand. And that was how he liked it. The church was easy to defend; difficult to attack. Even in his sickness he knew he had chosen his den well. And surely, it was the perfect place to hide his own cubs.

Lost within the permanent grey gloom, there were other foxes around him. Slivid stood closest, anxious but patient: certain that his fever would pass, that he would at last come back to her . . . Certain too that his tricks had worked, that no animal had seen through his disguises, that the town and all that went with the town was Skrinkle's for the taking. Their numbers were so few, the dogs and cats were so many, and yet without so much as a single fight he held the whole town between his open paws. *And* with an easy and abundant supply of meat to fill their larders.

"Rest my sweet, rest . . ." said Slivid. "And while you rest we'll let the sleeping dogs lie. They'll learn your ways, soon enough . . ."

And they learned. Oh yes, they learned . . .

Much later, and far above sleeping cats and dogs, Skrinkle-the-bird once more sat out upon his rooftop perch. He opened his wings, threw back his head and called out into the night. It was a long, low, triumphant screech that worried ears deep into the Outlands. Skrinkle was satisfied. It had been a good day. It had been a *very* good day . . . though he would not forget the six wary animals who had stood against him, almost upsetting his plans. Well, their time would come. He would see to it personally.

Twelve

Lambs to a Slaughter

Let the days pass. Let the scorching sun turn inevitably through the sky. Let full bellies begin to feel again the pangs of a desperate hunger.

Skrinkle's influence and power spread through the town faster than disease. He was the cunning one. Cunning and sly. The dogs and cats had been slowly starving to death, fighting among themselves for the few scraps of food to be had. When Skrinkle-the-fox had come, it had not been with bared teeth. No. He was far too clever for that. His weapons were food and water. His weapons were friendship and unity. How could any creature resist?

How easily, how cheaply, was loyalty bought. Having once been reminded of the joys of a full belly it was difficult for all but the most determined of starving cats and dogs to forget it again; to rely on their own wits to survive. For a few pieces of meat they sold their freedom to the foxes. Took Skrinkle's bait like fish to a hook. Allowed themselves to be fed and watered like the common man-pets so many of them had once been. Led like dull-brained sheep. If they had only understood . . .

Lambs to a slaughter.

From the day of the gorging, dogs and cats in countless numbers stayed permanently on the streets surrounding the foxes' den – ever hopeful of their next meal. And every so often – sometimes with a roar and a snort – the great wooden door of the church was flung open and down the stone steps came a procession of foxes. Always with Slivid walking at its head. Often with Skrinkle-the-bull or Skrinkle-the-bear walking, impressively, at her side. But as often without – when Skrinkle-the-bird would proudly fly the skies above them.

Other times, some town animal would glimpse a single dog or cat among the ranks of foxes. But just a glimpse, mind you, just a fleeting moment of recognition before the procession was hurried on past.

Rarest of all – and most hallowed – were the appearances of Skrinkle-the-fox. And then neither bull, nor bird nor any other creature but fox would show itself. He walked alone, always at the rear of the line. And with a lump of fresh meat held in his mouth, which he would solemnly bestow upon some poor half-starved wretch he happened upon along his way.

The processions always headed for the riverside, where they would come to a stop. And a great deal of time was spent bathing and drinking from the pool of water caught behind the makeshift dam. In time, around the margins of the pool the green shoots of new grass began to grow; enough even for the bull to feed upon when he had a mind.

And now you must ask, did it never seem strange to onlookers – to the many dogs and cats of the town – that neither Skrinkle-the-bull, nor Skrinkle-the-bird, nor Skrinkle-the-fox ever appeared *together*?

In truth . . . *no.*

Hunger and thirst are strange masters. Those poor animals chose not to see in Skrinkle's processions the trick that was being performed in front of them. They saw instead what they *wanted* to see in front of them: animals in unity, all shapes, all sizes, helping each other to survive. When the parading was done and the church door was closed against them, many an eager convert would creep closer to those stone steps desperate for Skrinkle's return . . .

And if there were a few wiser animals out on the streets who saw enough of the truth at least to wonder at the foxes' antics? They simply took the offered food and drink and slid into hiding, kept themselves alive and bided their time.

As for Skrinkle-the-fox, he knew that he alone could not hope to feed such a large number of animals for very long. Soon his rooftop store of food must fail him, and his regular feedings turn inevitably to regular slaughter.

Against obedient, trusting animals the act would be easily done.

Daily, the warrior bird would be seen in lone flight above the town. Always carefully watching. Noting which animal travelled where and with which animal. Noting the dogs and cats who threw in their lot with the foxes, and more importantly, noting those stubborn fools who did not; for it was these who were to be his first victims.

Thirteen

The Firing

Skrinkle-the-bird leapt from the roof of the church, beat his wings hard to gain height and soared out across a sharp, steel-blue sky. On the ground, his domination of the town centre was absolute; and the stupid creatures who prowled there still hardly knew it. But forget the streets, this day his concerns lay elsewhere—

With the slightest turn of a wing he wheeled down through the air and out across the barren river, plummeted until the wasted trees and grasses of the Town Moor swam up into focus. Then with a simple twist of his body he turned away and began to climb again. In that single sweep his eyes had seen enough, had found their prey. He saw Kim and Sleekit, Fisher and Saal, standing mute as stone watching after him. Saw Ki-ya and Dart break for cover, driving their companions before them, as he passed over their heads. He did not bother to attack. Six together – why put himself at risk of injury? The fools could neither hide from him nor outrun him. And there was an easier path to their destruction.

Upon the Outland hills he glimpsed the slight raft of smoke staining the sky and he remembered the crackle of stiff summer grass as it burned under the heat of the midday sun. Skrinkle-the-bird adored fire. He had often played in burning moorland. Thrilled at the ease at which he could lift the cold end of a withered stick while its hot end still burned. Thrilled at the way new fires would burst into life where burning sticks were dropped among dry grass . . .

* * *

Almost from the moment that Ki-ya and Dart had led their companions away from Skrinkle's gorging and returned to their familiar prowl upon the Town Moor they had noticed the eye of the warrior bird upon them. When he came looking, he flew a strict pattern. Broad looping circles that took him first deep into the Outlands and then back again across the town. Street by street, field by field. Backwards and forwards, forwards and backwards, the same flight over and over again. Sometimes, when he caught them walking out upon the open Town Moor, they would make a wild dash for deeper cover. But strangely, he never attacked, or changed his slow looping flight path.

What was he doing? They could not decide. Was he spying, or simply letting them know he was there? Or was there something else ... something far more sinister behind his comings and goings? They found out soon enough.

It happened on a day like any other day; already burning hot well before the sun had reached the top of the sky. The six animals were sitting together, as they often did, sheltering in the long dry grass at the fringes of a small wood. They saw the bird fly out across the river and disappear into the wilder countryside of the Outlands; beginning his daily routine. He reappeared a little later flying behind them as he completed his first looping circle. Then he began all over again, gliding off across the river and back over the streets of the town.

The bird completed his monotonous routine three times without variation. But on the fourth, when it was time for him to reappear, he did not come.

"Sister, where has our spy got to?" asked Ki-ya, only half-interested.

"Pah! Who cares?" laughed Dart. "Hopefully he's crash-landed into a tree and broken his neck!" Kim and Sleekit tried to laugh with her. But they did care. As time passed without sight of the bird, they became uneasy, their ears stood upright and alert, tails twisted thoughtfully. Unwisely, they found themselves prowling out on to the open Moor. And a desperate curiosity kept them there, far longer than was safe.

Suddenly, there he was, flying at them out of nowhere, moving very fast and low. His wings beating fiercely, driving the air behind him. A streak of scorched wind through the midday sky.

"Quickly, now, take cover, he's coming straight for us! He's attacking!" cried Dart, trying to bully Fisher and Saal into action.

"No, Dart, no he's not — See?" yapped the pup. The bird did not swoop to the kill. He kept on going, flew right over their heads and into the woods behind them.

"He's carrying something between his claws," said Sleekit, perplexed.

"Carrying what?" asked Kim, his old eyes

seeing only the blur of movement. "Some piece of rancid carrion?"

"No. No, not meat — But he *is* carrying something, and I don't like it." In the wake of the bird, instead of clear blue sky, there was the oddest trail; a grey smudge clinging to the air, marking out his flight path. And with it came the faintest of smells, that tickled the nose and made them sneeze.

"Smoke," said Ki-ya. "He's carrying smoke."

"What?" cried Dart at the impossibility of it all.

"Yes! Yes — See! A stick. Between his claws – a burning stick!"

To those animals smoke and fire meant very little; it had always been something of a mystery. Between them, they had seen it often enough and in many of its guises: billowing smoke from factory chimneys; the lashing flames of allotment bonfires; the gentle warmth of a fireside hearth; and the distant burning of moorland deep within the

Outlands. But, as fire had never done them any harm, it did not worry them. They did not understand how an untamed fire worked – its lethal threat, its awesome powers of destruction.

As they watched, the trail of smoke behind the bird dipped out of the sky.

"He's dropped it. The bird's dropped his smoking stick in among the trees," said Kim.

"Ki-ya, I don't understand," said Dart. "What does he think he's doing?"

Ki-ya had no answer.

Skrinkle-the-bird turned upon the air, and still moving at great speed, headed back the way he had come. Backwards and forwards he flew, and each time he returned, a thin plume of smoke drifted behind him. Again and again he dropped his burning embers. Sometimes they fell in among the wood behind them, sometimes out on the Town Moor in front of them. The wind was blowing, carrying the smoke their way, but nothing else seemed to be happening.

Intrigued, but still unworried, dogs and cats calmly sat down to watch the bird's strange antics.

And then, on Skrinkle's next run, something changed. He dropped his burning stick just the same as before, but this time the smoke drifting back off the ground was instantly more than the thin vaporous trail going down. Then, for a moment, there was no smoke at all, as if something had got in its way. Then it came again, and heavier; thick billowing clouds drifted out over the Town Moor, blotting out the sun, and with it came a sound like the monstrous rumbling purr of some incredible giant beast.

The bird did not stop to look or listen. He flew off again, came back again, dropped another plume of smoke into the woods behind them. There was another instant black cloud of belching smoke, and the roaring of a second monster.

Cats' fur bristled. They spat and hissed. Dogs' ears stood urgently erect, and a deep guttural snarl rose up in Kim's throat as if in warning. What was happening to the Town Moor? The thickening veil of smoke was moving rapidly closer. Stalking them almost, and on two – no, three sides already, as if it was deliberately trying to hem them in.

Without a word, each of them turned and bolted for the wood. Though not before they'd left the sweet stain of fear on the ground behind them.

The wood; cats could always lose themselves in the wood, it had long been their sanctuary, their safe haven. No man or predator had ever come close to finding them there. And what it did for them, surely it could do just as well for the dogs.

If only they had understood fire. How quickly, how easily it moved. There it was already, in front of them as they ran in between the trees. The grey veil of smoke. The roar of the wild beast. And with it came an unbearable heat from a stolen sun. It scorched their fur and blistered their noses and tongues as the beast drew breath. How completely it devoured everything that stood in its way.

Instinctively, Ki-ya jumped for the branches of a tree, but its bark sparked red and a roaring flame licked at tinder-dry branches. He leapt to the ground again, only to find the withered grass burning beneath his paws.

The fire closed in, tightened its grip. And beneath the twisting wreaths of black smoke he lost all sight of Kim and Sleekit. Heard only a distant shriek that might have been poor Saal crying for his mother. Then, for a moment, there was Dart's tail—

"Follow me! This way, brother! Make for the road. See? The road does not burn yet—!"

"But it's *behind* the wall of fire—!" Their only way of escape lay through the flames, through the consuming belly of the fire beast.

"Yes, yes!"

"I — I can't." Ki-ya hesitated, stricken with fear; for the first time in all his life, his courage failed him.

"Brother, we must! And we must move now, or die!" Dart opened her claws and drew blood from Ki-ya's shoulder. It was enough to pull him out of his stupor.

Together, with a defiant squeal, Ki-ya and Dart ran into the wall of flame.

Open-winged and gliding easily upon a rising wind, Skrinkle-the-bird looked down and saw Ki-ya and Dart running panic-stricken into the fire. He screeched his contempt at their ignorance, his call full of laughter as the wind drove the flames before it. The fire seemed to bite chunks out of the wood as it passed through the trees, and left nothing standing in its wake. He turned a slow, easy circle across the sky, watched as the fire moved safely away from the town. His work was done. Soon he would glide back across the river to rest upon his beloved church tower. There was no point in searching out the bodies of the dead: there would be little enough to find; no meat fit for the eating (and there was plenty more where that came from).

PART TWO

Fourteen

Bryna and the Mad Dog

And now, for a short while, we must look back down a road we have already long since travelled; to the day of the singing wire fence and the green metal men with their guns. And there, where others failed, *we* must find blind Bryna, wandering alone, lost deep within the Outlands. Heedless of direction, unsure of her footing, of the landscape that faces her. She often stumbles, often falls, only to force herself back on to her feet again. And where is she running to? She does not know. There is only a deepening hunger sickness. Only a raging thirst; and the violent sting of pain in her backside where the soldier's bullet had torn off her tail. Only a mindless confusion . . .

She was certain she had called out to her companions; to Ki-ya, and to the old mongrel, Kim. Inside her head she had even called upon her ghosts for help. But none had come to her this time. None had come.

At first she had kept close to the singing wire fence. Its soft melancholic song was always there to keep her company; and to warn her off. And better the enemy she knew . . . But eventually the twists and turns of the hillside had carried her away from it, until it was so distant she could no longer hear its call.

At one point the stiff dead grass under her paws suddenly turned into an uneven bed of broken stones and small pebbles. Then as quickly into hard-baked, compacted soil. And then into the artificial tarmac of a narrow road.

Confusion upon confusion.

Without thinking, she turned along it,

began to follow its length, using the touch of her paws to guide her: trusted that road to take her down off the hillside and back into the river valley she knew.

It was a false hope. What she did not know – in her confusion could not have known – was that this road was leading her farther and farther *away* from her river, not towards it: taking her deeper and deeper into the unknown Outlands. She was too tired now, too stricken with fear, ill with hunger and dehydration to puzzle it out.

It was then, through her feverish panic, that she began to sense a change in the landscape around her. Suddenly, the open countryside of the Outlands didn't feel quite so open. Something was throwing long shadows across the road and there were the faintest of smells; smells she associated with the streets and the buildings of men.

That was it—! There *were* buildings close by now. Though not enough to have the makings of a town; the weight they rested upon her mind was too slight for that. She guessed it was more like a single row of houses, or at most a gathering of two or three streets set, higgledly-piggledly, against the twists and turns of the road.

After only a few dozen paces the shadows across the road fell away, and the countryside opened up again. She might have left it all behind her then, gone on until she finally dropped with exhaustion, except that the slightest of sounds reached her ears.

Scrat-a-pat, scrat-a-pat.

She stood still, lifted her ears and listened. But whatever animal had made the noise, it seemed it knew she was listening and fell instantly silent.

Slowly, Bryna turned around in the road, took a few short steps; enough to take her back into the shadows of the houses.

There it was again: scrat-a-pat, scrat-a-pat.

The noise came from somewhere up above

her – surely, from a rooftop – and lasted only long enough for a lone animal to find its footing.

"Who's there?" Bryna found the strength to call. "There's no point in hiding." There was no answer. So, she moved forward an extra few strides, hoped the curiosity of the watcher would get the better of it. It did.

Scrat-a-pat, scrat-a-pat.

"Who is it—? I know you're up there. And if this is an ambush you'd better get on with it. I don't have the strength left for a fight. Can't even see you. I'm blind."

Silence . . . The watcher was thinking. Trying to make up its mind about something.

"You go your way, cat. You're not a proper customer. It's ours and you're not havin' any of it, missus."

"Customer? Having any of it? Having any of what?" asked Bryna.

"Don't play the innocent with me," said the watcher. "I says to myself, I says, Mr

Edwards, I've seen her type before. Trying it on with her tricks an' lies. If I come down off this garage roof to help you, your mates will only come rushing out of their hiding-places, ganging up on me. So, like I said, go your way, you're not having any of it."

Bryna's damaged tail flicked feebly with annoyance at the animal's curious jibber-jabber. And the sudden extra stab of pain it gave only served to make her even more annoyed. "I don't know *what* you're talking about—" she spat and hissed as loudly as she could.

"Likely story. I says to myself, I says, she'll be after pinching our stock. Probably one of them lot that comes skulking around in the middle of the night. Well, I'm telling you, there ain't none. Not for your sort."

Bryna managed another weak mew, but with that she felt herself falling over. In the event she did not pass out, or at least if she did it was only for a moment. She found herself lying in the middle of the road, stricken. Too miserable, too weak and feeble to do anything about it.

It was a very long time before the watcher called out again. As if he was satisfying himself that Bryna's collapse wasn't just another clever trick.

"You dead, cat? You a goner, missus?" In a very deliberate, much practised way, Mr Edwards shuffled to the edge of his garage roof and leapt to the ground. He walked slowly and carefully into the middle of the road, began snuffling around Bryna's neck and head, licking at her nose tentatively, as if he still expected some sudden attack.

"No, I'm not dead. Not yet," Bryna hissed weakly. She raised a paw to fend him off and at last began to smell him for what he was . . . *A dog.* There was a stale smell about him; not unhealthy, but a mixture of old age, bad teeth and bad diet.

"Not a gang, or a shoplifter?"

"A what—? No—"

"Not after our stock, then?"

"No!"

"Aye, well, you're in a bit of a mess though, aren't you, missus? Still, you can't blame me for being careful, not in this day and age." The dog looked about furtively, and then began to whisper in Bryna's ear. "Our stock's a bit of a secret, see. Kept it to ourselves all this time ... in case the customers come back. Always got to be ready in case there's customers to serve."

Bryna had already decided; the dog was obviously mad. A loony; completely off his head! It sometimes happens that way with old dogs, or dogs left without company, too long on their own.

"If it's all the same to you, I'd rather be left alone to die in peace," she said.

"Oh ... Still dying is it?" The dog sat down quietly, as if he was thinking even more carefully about something. Then at last he said, "Aye . . . Of course, that would mean you'd be missing out on our summer sale."

"Summer sale?" repeated Bryna. The dog was talking gibberish again.

"Extra-special offers, missus. Bargains galore. One day only—! You could take a hold of my tail if you like, and I'll lead you to it."

If she'd had the strength, she would have backed away from him. But she did not. Not the strength to run away, not the strength to argue any more. Bryna struggled to stand up, using his lowered tail clenched between her teeth as support. Mr Edwards was a very big muscular dog, with a long, thick mane of golden-brown hair (if only she could have seen it).

She allowed him to lead her off the road and towards the houses, felt the shadows deepen across her back as they moved past a line of sheltered doorways. In one doorway,

Mr Edwards stopped. And there a very simple, but wonderful thing happened . . .

The dog opened the door.

The dog opened the *closed* door.

She felt his powerful front paws running up its wooden panels until he was standing upright; heard his teeth and jaws working hard, scraping against a metal handle or latch there, until it gave way and the door swung open. As it did, somewhere close by a small bell rang *ting-a-ting*. Bryna let go of his tail, decided she could still manage to stand on her own four paws after all. There was obviously more to this mad dog than the smell that met her nose.

"Come on in, then, come on in," Mr Edwards insisted.

"But how, how did you do that?"

"Ah—, well. Opening doors is a secret too, see. Handed down through the generations, from father to son, like . . ." He looked down at Bryna, wanted her to be impressed. She was. He whispered, "It's all in the handle, missus." As if that explained everything.

"Sorry?"

"Handles," he repeated. "Handles and locks, that is. Some doors are closed with handles, some are closed with locks. The secret is in understanding the difference."

"Is there a difference?" As far as Bryna was concerned a closed door was a closed door and that was that. She had come up against enough of them in her time.

"*Is* there a difference! My dear cat . . ." His tail wagged frantically, but he didn't explain himself any further. Instead he lowered his head and nudged Bryna through the open door and into the room behind it.

The instant stale, closed-in stuffiness reminded Bryna of the house she had once shared with the old woman, Mrs Ida Tupps. But, quite unexpectedly, the air was also filled with the most tantalising mixture of potent smells she had ever come across in one place.

Bryna sniffed deeply, using her tongue to taste the air. Impossible though it was, the room behind the door was full of things to eat.

And then it finally dawned on her . . .

This house was what men called a corner shop. She had only vague memories of shops. Of course her town had once been full of them . . . still was, in a way. But of all men's buildings their shops were the most securely closed, and the best-protected against unwanted intruders. No open windows there, no doors left carelessly ajar. Iron grilles and closed steel shutters mostly, or else whole walls of solid glass far too thick for any cat or dog to break. (Not that that had stopped many an animal from trying in the early days; tearing their claws out, beating themselves senseless against it.) Eventually, the shops had come to be left well alone; just another part of the impenetrable wall of man-made mountains that made up much of the town. Best forgotten about, or left to the late night fairy tales of elderly dogs and cats who would tell of huge rooms stuffed to the ceiling with food, of strange magical boxes endlessly full of fresh, sweet-tasting meats. And the more the stories were told, the more far-fetched they became until even the animals who remembered the real shops did not believe in them.

Mr Edwards snuffled about among his boxes of stock. Pushing his nose between the rows of shelves that lined the walls, and into the open steel cabinet that stood in the middle of the floor.

"Of course, a lot of it's gone off a bit now—" he said. There were some very old, mouldy green stains gathered like furry puddles around the bottom of the cabinet. "But not the dry packets, or the glass jars, or the tins. And you can still eat the best of the chocolate . . . You'll find the cardboard boxes easiest to open at first; you just have to give them a good tug with your teeth. Whereas your jars are a little more tricky. I says to myself, I says, got to be broken, they have. Got to pick your way carefully through the bits of glass. But it was the tins I had the *real* bother with at first . . ."

Bryna wasn't really listening to him. Her head was turning woozily in circles, her nose stinging hot with the sudden bombardment of smells.

"Now you just take your time, browse all you like, missus. There are plenty of free samples to help you choose." Mr Edwards stood up on his hind legs and nosed one of the cardboard packets off the wooden counter. Its contents spilled out across the floor. "Go on, now, help yourself. I don't know *exactly* what it is, but you can eat it."

The dog might be barking mad, but Bryna did not need a second invitation. She snuffled the strange dry mixture into her mouth as best she could. It was almost tasteless and gave her no pleasure. And yet somehow, it quickly filled her empty belly in a strangely satisfying way.

"Steady, now, steady, missus. Don't go stuffing it all in in one go. You'll be needing yourself a drink of water with that; if you don't want your belly to explode on you."

"Water?" Bryna couldn't have been more surprised.

"Of course, water. Now, there's always the bottled variety—" He stopped and thought a moment. "But you come with me. I'm sure you'd like to take it straight from the tap, eh?" Mr Edwards reached up to the handle of a door at the back of the shop and pulled it open. Behind it was a narrow hallway, with more doors that lead to the living rooms of the house and a single flight of stairs. "We'll have to be quiet though . . . Sugar'll still be having her nap around this time."

"Sugar?" asked Bryna. Could there really be more than one mad dog in the house?

"Aye, missus, my er, my own missus, if you'll s'cuse the pun. She doesn't get about much . . . on account of her legs. I'll take you in to see her when she wakes, if you like?"

The upstairs of the house was even more like Bryna's old home with Mrs Ida Tupps than the downstairs. There were five rooms altogether; three large bedrooms (one, she supposed, with Sugar lying asleep in it), plus a tiny room only big enough for a toilet, and a bathroom.

Could Bryna believe her ears? From the bathroom there came the very gentle tip-i-tap-tip of water dripping.

"Now, turning on taps took me some learning, I can tell you, missus – broke more than a couple of teeth on those I have. But I got there in the end. As far as I can figure it, the water comes down from up out of the roof, but don't ask me how.

Every house in Fenholm has given me more than a bath full—"

"Fenholm?"

"Aye, missus. Where you are – village of Fenholm. Anyway, like I says, every house has given me a bath full. Of course, what with all this drought, it's been getting a bit low . . ."

Bryna stopped listening again and jumped head-first into the bath without waiting to be asked. Her paws slid awkwardly across its smooth enamel surface, and she found herself lying sprawled, ungainly, in a thin puddle of water that was trapped at the very bottom. She did not care about the indignity of it, and lapped frantically at the cool clear liquid.

When she had finished, she lifted her head self-consciously, sensed that Mr Edwards was looking down at her over the side of the bath. "Oh, by the way," she said, suddenly bold, "my name's not Missus, it's Bryna."

"Aye, that'll be right," he said. "That'll be right, missus."

The days that followed, living over the corner shop with the mad Mr Edwards, were to be a strange but happy time for Bryna. She became used to his ways. To his pretence at being human. To eating his dry food out of packets; she soon learned how to break them open by gnawing at the cardboard until it became soggy and dissolved in her mouth. And to his foolish game with Sugar . . .

It's not that there was no Sugar. There was. And she was confined to her bed, just as he had said—

"She's perhaps still asleep," whispered Mr Edwards, as he lead Bryna cautiously through the bedroom door. "Aye . . . still asleep. We'll not disturb her." The room was in constant darkness, with the curtains at the small window always pulled firmly closed. Sugar was hidden beneath a large blanket on the bed. Bryna lifted her nose to the air and tried to sense out the second dog. The air smelled musty and very dry. But there was no new animal scent. And there was no weight of thought trying to find her mind. Mr Edward's charade was for the benefit of those with eyes.

"Um?"

"Just say hello, if you like," he whispered. "She's a bit on the deaf side is Sugar, so she'll maybe not hear you, but you can give it a try."

"Um . . . hello, Sugar," Bryna said slowly, still puzzled. She jumped up on to the bed.

There was no other dog in the room. Not alive. Not dead even. But there was *something*, something large and stiff, bristle-haired and dog-shaped tucked snugly under the blanket. Sugar was a human kitten's stuffed toy—

A toy dog.

Later, and unabashed, Mr Edwards took great pride in showing Bryna how he had solved the problem of opening tin cans. First, he took his chosen tin in his mouth, lifted it down off the shop shelf, and carried it all the way up the stairs to the toilet. There he jumped up on to the toilet seat, raised himself up on his hind legs and dropped the tin out through a small broken pane of glass in the window. There was a dull metallic clack as the tin buckled against the concrete of the back yard. Mr Edwards bounded happily down the stairs and, with a great deal of excited tail-wagging, ran around to the back of the shop to retrieve the dented can.

He went through the whole process again; carried the tin back up the stairs, threw it back out of the window. Waited for the telling thud. Then he did it *all* again. Until, on the fourth or fifth attempt, the tin hitting the concrete rang a different, broken note. The tin had finally split open, and its contents spilled out. Something brown and vaguely meat-like oozed across the ground.

This was the cause for much celebration, and even more wild excitement. Mr Edwards chased the broken can madly around the back yard, pushing it backwards and forwards with his nose as if he was a pup again playing with his first ball. Then, with great ceremony, he invited Bryna to taste the spillings, before joining in himself, full of joyous abandonment.

Most of their days were spent either sitting in the armchairs in the small living-room behind the shop or else serving in the shop (which, as far as Bryna could tell, amounted to taking very long lazy naps lying on the shop counter or on the mat in front of the shop door). There were never any customers.

Generally, they ate their meals wherever

they fell from the packets or tins. But sometimes, when the mood struck him, Mr Edwards would insist on carrying the food to the kitchen table and they would sit around on dining chairs eating their meals off a plate as best they could.

Sugar, of course, never joined them for their meals.

"Prefers her own company," said Mr Edwards. "On account of her teeth."

"Teeth?" said Bryna.

"Ain't got none, missus."

"Ah," said Bryna, knowingly.

Of all their times spent together, Bryna's favourite was the cool of the evening, just before the sun went down. Mr Edwards would take her on a slow walk through the few short empty streets that made up their small village. A stroll he called it. And as they walked they talked. He told her wonderful stories of life in Fenholm before men abandoned it. Of real customers. Wholesalers.

Bakers. Butchers. Smelly iron lorries stuffed full of fresh meat. And stories about Sugar when she was young and fit; playing wild games of catch-me-if-you-can with human kittens in the street. *Before* she took to her bed. In return Bryna would try to scare him with tales of her ghosts, which (although he protested) he liked best of all.

Their walks always ended at an ancient rusting metal road machine. A car, that sat at the kerb side at the back of the shop; its windscreen missing, and one door fixed permanently open, held out like the broken wing of a bird. *His* car, Mr Edwards insisted. They would sit inside, and the mad dog would pretend to take her for a drive . . . He could even make the car *go* by releasing the hand brake with his teeth; it would lurch a few paws' lengths forward before shuddering to a stop again.

At night they slept upstairs in their own bedrooms, with soft mattresses, pillows and blankets. Once or twice, in the very early hours, Bryna clearly heard the scratting of paws at the shop door. Mr Edwards would bark out, "Night visitors." Then he would prowl through the house and shop alone, gently growling to himself until the noises outside stopped and the unwelcome visitors slipped away into the night. Nothing more ever came of it.

And so, with regular meals and the simple routine of shop life, Bryna quickly regained her old strength and body weight. She took easily to the lazy, man-like way of doing things. Even found herself having brief conversations with the stuffed toy that was Sugar. She might have lived out her days there, might have forgotten old troubles, old friends.

But it was all to end soon enough . . .

Sugar died.

Fifteen

Sugar's Funeral

"I found her just the way she is," said Bryna, honestly enough. And then her first lie. "She must have slipped away peacefully in the night."

Sugar lay on her bed, undisturbed in death. There had been no sudden, meaningless act of violence. No bloody argument. No desperate wild pursuit by foraging hunters. She was simply a very old dog and her time had come. At least, that was what Bryna told Mr Edwards. One lie upon another. And she felt sick with the guilt of it. But what choice was there? Sugar's death was the only way—

As time had passed, Bryna had begun to

notice that regular meals were becoming less regular. That portions were becoming smaller, and drinks of water less generous. The shop was running out of stock. The shop was running out of stock and Mr Edwards refused to see it.

At best there was a few days' worth of food and drink left. If Bryna had not come up with *something* the mad dog would have gone on pretending until it was too late. Until he was as dead as the piece of stuffed cotton that lay on his bed: and Bryna dead with him.

"She was a good old girl," said Mr Edwards, "never asked for much . . ." But there was no brave face. His huge head, his tail, his whole body seemed to hang down, lifelessly. His golden fur instantly lost its shine and became full of tats and knots that had to be bitten out with his teeth. It was as if something in her death had killed a part of him too.

He hauled himself on to Sugar's bed, settled himself next to her body and refused to move. Not to eat or drink, not even to open up his precious shop to his non-existent customers. His grief was almost worse than his madness! Now he was going to starve himself to death while there was still food to be eaten!

But if Sugar's fake death made a difference to Mr Edwards, it also made a difference to Bryna. Strangely, it unsettled her. It was ever a cat's way to think of itself first – such was survival – but now she remembered the town. *Her* town. She remembered the drought, the starvation, the futile fighting, and the endless suffering of animals there. Most important of all – and with a sickening realisation – she began to see that there was an answer to that suffering and she had known it from her very first meeting with the mad dog. It was time to leave the shop, it was time for them both to leave . . . If only she could persuade him.

"Come now, Mr Edwards, what about the . . . *the arrangements*?" Bryna began, tentatively. "The – er – the *funeral* arrangements?"

The dog's ears pricked. "Pardon?"

"Well, you can't put it off forever. I mean, there is going to be a proper funeral and – er – everything. You know, *a proper burial*? Sugar wouldn't have put up with anything less . . . There's the grave to dig, and the flowers to um, to um — Oh, and the headstone to plant." Bryna didn't know *very* much about human funerals (only what she had picked up from Treacle, who'd spent much of a past winter living alone in a graveyard). Luckily, Mr Edwards knew even less.

At last the mad dog sat up. Almost as if he had suddenly come back to life.

Sugar was buried in a shallow hole, dug out of the one narrow strip of ground in the backyard that was not solid concrete. Her headstone was a worn house brick (an old plaything of Mr Edwards). Her flowers a bunch of plastic daffodils that had stood in a vase in the middle of the kitchen table. Mr Edwards insisted on moving Sugar's body on his own, and late at night, and would not let Bryna near the grave until the thing was done . . .

"I want you to come back to my town with me," Bryna said quietly to Mr Edwards, when at last it was all over.

"You mean, you mean, you want me to leave my home, and my shop . . . and poor, Sugar?"

"Yes, yes, I do. Mr Edwards, you have skills I have never seen in any animal before. Don't you see? All across my town there are shops and houses just like yours . . . Hundreds of them! The trouble is most of their doors are closed against me, and I can't open them. I can't. But you can. *You can*—!

"There are dogs and cats starving to death when there's more food and drink shut away inside the buildings that surround them, than they could all of them possibly eat in a lifetime. In nine lifetimes!" She hesitated a moment, hoped the idea would sink in. "And what is there left here for you? It's too late for Sugar, but just think of the lives you *could* save."

The dog said nothing, stared hopelessly at the ground.

Bryna tried again. "You, you could open a new shop – a whole chain of shops! And with real live customers too—"

Mr Edwards shuffled about a bit, looked down at the grey patch of bare earth that marked Sugar's grave. "Oh, I see . . . you mean it's a sort of business proposition. Yes, well . . . it is very tempting, isn't it, dear?" he said to the ground. "But you know, this little shop is all we ever needed. Besides, I says to myself, I says, who would look after *our* customers when they come back? No. No, if it's all the same to you; no thank you, missus."

Bryna was at her wits' end.

"Your shop stock is getting very low. You've been trying to hide it from me, but I've noticed. I might be blind, but my paws know an empty shelf when they walk it."

"Well, Bryna, it's very nice of you to be worried about us, but we'll be all right. We belong here, don't we, Sugar? It's been wonderful having you to stay, but if it's time for you to be off home then we understand."

Enough was enough. "Listen! Oh please, *listen* to me, you mad old fool! Sugar was a — Sugar was a bloody—"

"Yes, missus?"

Bryna could hardly bring herself to say it "Sugar was a bloody silly—"

And then, suddenly, there in front of her stood Grundle, her own dead Grundle. He had not come to her in all this time and yet, there he was; shaking his head, smiling sadly at the way she had lost her temper, his sparrow sitting on his shoulder shaking its head with him. He was only there a moment, but long enough to stop Bryna from shouting, long enough to cast a shadow across her mind, and to give her a new idea.

"Mr Edwards, I've got to tell you something . . . Sugar is here. She's here, right now, standing next to me."

"W-what?"

"I mean, I mean her ghost is here. That's it, her ghost. And she says . . . she says she's very happy, and she says she's healthy, and you must not worry about her. Oh, and, and she says she wants you to come back to the town with me . . ." Her words had a thin empty ring to them that would not have convinced any but the maddest of animals. Bryna had *never* lied about her ghosts before. She was no fake. But she lied then, lied for all she was worth, because he would not listen to the truth. And, well, she just couldn't think of another way of persuading him.

Sixteen

Strange Meeting

The following morning, Bryna and Mr Edwards left the corner shop together; with the sound of its little bell ting-a-tinging in their ears as the door swung closed behind them for the last time.

Was it a fool's errand? Maybe Bryna was mad, just like the dog, for even trying? Finding her way back to the town would not be easy. She did not know which way to travel or how far they must go. Bryna had only two vague notions, which did not add up to very much. The first was to stick to the roads, leaving Fenholm along the same narrow country lane by which she had first come into it. The second was always to walk away from the heat of the sun in the mornings and always towards it in the afternoons.

They walked all that day, stopping only tentatively, every now and then, to take a little food or water. Mr Edwards had insisted on filling a plastic bag with groceries, from the last of the shop supplies, which he carried by its handles between his teeth. There was bottled water, a full packet of dried food, and the last few pieces of chocolate.

They did not stop to sleep until the very last glow of orange light from a fading sun disappeared from the evening sky. (Once, during the night, the feeble death squeal of some poor animal and the urgent clap-flapping of a hunting bird's wings cracked the uneasy silence, startling them awake. But nothing more came of it.) They were on the move again at first light, and stuck rigidly to the twisting line of their country lane.

Every so often they came upon cross-roads, where one narrow lane met another. And ever hopeful, Bryna would face the sun before deciding which way they should take. It came as quite a shock to discover she could actually sense which was the right way to go without ever having been there before. And when, late that second morning, their tiny country lane disappeared under a huge four-lane dual carriageway, bullying its way through the Outlands like a swollen stone river, she was almost expecting it.

And then, for the very first time since setting out, Bryna sensed the movement of an animal on the road ahead of them. It was a long way off, and vague among the fierce squalls of rising hot air, but it was definitely an animal; a lone animal coming their way.

"Outlander, no doubt—" growled Mr Edwards. "Night prowler. And one of your own, missus. A cat."

"A cat—?"

"Aye. And a fighting cat by the looks of it."

It was. And although its movement was heavy and laboured, it was walking carelessly down the centre of the road, making no attempt to conceal itself.

Well, blind or not, if she was forced, Bryna could still make a fight of it. And Mr Edwards might be mad, but he was big strong dog.

Her broken tail began to swing in warning.

But then she began to hear the catching of a gasping breath, to smell the peculiar sourness of the cat's body scent, to taste its fear upon her tongue. There was something very *very* wrong with this animal. Bryna's tail stopped swinging. She stood still, warned Mr Edwards to do the same. "Let it come to us . . ."

As the cat came closer it began to call

feebly to her. "Bryna? Oh Bryna, is it really you?"

Bryna's heart leapt, and she could not help a deep rolling purr rising in her throat. Walking towards her was Dart. Dart in such an evil, distressed state, Bryna had simply not recognised her.

What terrible thing, what terrible, unspeakable thing had happened? Why did her body reek so much of fear? And where was her brother, where was Ki-ya? Surely he could not be very far away? She lifted her ears and nose to the air, searching for signs of his presence.

All that came to her were the foul smells that clung about Dart, disguising her familiar scents: bitter, pungent smells, that closed the nose and brought stomach bile to her throat. The smell of burning. The smell of wood smoke. The smell of brutal fire.

And if Bryna only sensed Dart's fear and distress, Mr Edwards saw it too, and cried out loud in pity. Dart's body would not settle, jumped and twitched in obvious agony. Her fur was burned black, in places stripped away completely around deep open sores that could not bare the slightest touch from a soothing tongue — But enough . . .

"Dart, my Dart, what has happened? And where is Ki-ya?" Bryna asked, frantic now. "Where are Sleekit and Kim? Fisher and her pup?"

Dart's head hung low; she could not lift her eyes, not even to look upon blind Bryna's face.

"Ki-ya . . . is dead . . ." She hesitated, the words had come out too easily, and surely meant nothing. "Bryna, Ki-ya is dead . . . and for all I know the others lie dead with him."

They spent that night together, upon the very spot where they had met. Mr Edwards fed them with packet food and bottled water from his plastic bag, and they ate and drank in vacant silence.

When the moon stood up high and bright against a black star-marked sky and turned the distant hills of the Outlands to silver, they did not even notice.

At length, out of the silence, Bryna found a voice to speak with. She reminded them first of their doomed adventure together. Of the battle at the singing wire fence. Of their forced separation and desperate escape. And of the cruel way the green metal men had taken both Lugger's and Treacle's bodies. Then she spoke of better days. Of her meeting with Mr Edwards and Sugar. Of their easy life together in the shop. And of their determination now to use Mr Edwards' secret skill at opening doors to find them food and water, to save the animals of the town from certain death . . .

Bryna's news should have given Dart new hope. But it did not. Ki-ya's death, the uncertain absence of so many others, was a weight that hung too heavily about them to be talked away.

Dart only shook her head sadly, winced with the constant cruel pain that would not leave her damaged body alone, and steeled herself to tell her own story. If Bryna's adventures were not strange enough, she could not have guessed at the horrors Dart had to tell. Of the coming of the foxes, Skrinkle and Slivid, to the town, and the foolish, blind turning of so many cats and dogs their way. Of the damming of the river and the gorging. Of the parading of the giant bull from the church den. Of the strange warrior bird who flew constantly overhead, spying on them all. And, of course, of the killing fires he made.

Seventeen

Bryna's Nightmare

Surely, this was the worst of all the times Bryna had ever known.

And what were they to do now? Just when she thought she had found in Mr Edwards the solution to the drought – an abundant source of food and water – what did she have instead? Their town under the rule of some tyrannical fox, and overrun with strange, wild animals. Ki-ya was dead. Dart so badly injured it was a miracle she had survived. And Kim and Sleekit, Fisher and Saal? Who could say?

For a long time that night Bryna lay awake, fretting. (While at her side, Dart moaned gently with every breath she took; as if to soothe the raw, weeping burns on her poor body.)

When at last she did fall asleep, it was a strange sleep with the most awful, vivid nightmares; full of wild, murderous beasts who chased her mercilessly across the town, across the Outlands. They flew, they ran, they crawled after her on their bellies. And when at last the beasts knew they could not catch her, they began to laugh scornfully, and took bites out of their own flesh to feed their hunger, even as it killed them.

And then, in among the nightmares, Bryna's ghosts came to her once again.

"Well, isn't this a fine pickle for a pussy-cat?" There was dead Grundle walking slowly out of the night towards her. On his shoulder his bird was singing happily to itself, unconcerned.

"Help me," said Bryna, her voice such a thin squeak she did not recognise it. "Please help me. Tell me what I must do."

"What's to do, eh? What's to do . . . Well, what would Grundle have done? Turned himself around? Gone back the way he'd come?

Found himself some other place to live. Why get yourself killed when there's already been enough killing? Isn't that the way of it?"

"What—! That might be *your* way. Looking after yourself, first and last. But it's not mine. It's not mine!" Even in her sleep Bryna felt her hackles rise.

The ghost cat wasn't in the least bit offended. "It seems to me you've got yourself an awful lot of enemies and very few friends, pussy-wussy," he said. "At least, very few live ones! Aye, and maybe you're asking your question of the wrong cat—"

The sparrow cack-cackered, suddenly distracted, lost its footing and with a flutter of wings fell off dead Grundle's back.

Standing behind the ghost was another tom cat now. A younger cat. Almost his size. Almost his colour. But a vague phantom still, hardly more solid than the shadows of the night.

Bryna's fur stood upon end; not with fear, but with a tingle of excitement.

"Ki-ya," whispered Bryna. "My Ki-ya, can that be you?"

"Why ever not, pussy-cat," said Grundle, purring. "Why ever not?"

The shadows began moving awkwardly towards her, as if even in death Ki-ya still hobbled upon three paws. "Listen to me, Bryna, listen. This is what you must do: bring together the worst of all your enemies—"

"What? But—"

"You have neither the strength of body nor the strength of numbers to make a fight of it. So – you must bring the worst of your enemies together and let *them* fight. Let one destroy the other!"

"Ki-ya, I don't understand – the *worst* of my enemies? Isn't this world full of my enemies?"

As Bryna spoke, Grundle played with two small stones between his paws. He pushed them deliberately apart, brought them deliberately together again. "Use your nose, pussy-cat. Isn't that the scent of poor Dart's burned body that carries upon the night air? Wasn't this a bird's doing; the servant of a certain fox—?"

"And do not forget the sting in your own tail!" said Ki-ya.

"Then you mean . . . you mean *fox*, and *man*?"

"Aye . . . Skrinkle and your soldiers, your green metal men."

"But Ki-ya, how can it possibly be done?"

"You must find a way. Return to the town and *find* a way . . . And when you need us, call for us. Call for the dead and we will come—"

Bryna woke up with a start. Ghosts and nightmares were gone; and explanations gone with them.

Eighteen

House-hunting

The early morning sun shocked the world with its brightness, chased away the night sky and with it the dreams and nightmares of sleeping animals.

Sitting out upon the dual carriageway, blind Bryna tried hard to recall her own particular nightmare. Insisted on telling Dart and Mr Edwards every little detail. All about the wriggling beasts and her ghosts; and the strange task she had been set.

"Ki-ya told me to return to the town. And well . . . he said I must bring the fox, Skrinkle, and the green metal men face to face. He said I must make them fight each other. It is the only way of ridding ourselves of either."

None of it seemed remotely possible. She had only hoped that talk of seeing Ki-ya's ghost would help lift Dart's spirits.

It did not. Dart sat looking vacantly at her. Unable to steady her nerves enough to stop the constant trembling of her injured body. "Pah! Talking to dead cats. Where's the sense in that?" She was not the fighting wild cat Bryna had once known, and she had never been one for ghosts.

Mr Edwards tried wagging his tail in moral support, but Dart only gave him a withering look, so he stopped.

"It's all very well going back to the town, but what happens when Skrinkle's great warrior bird or some other of his wild creatures comes searching us out? How can we begin to plot such a battle when we can't even keep ourselves alive? You've had a bad dream Bryna, that's all – let's leave it at that."

"But Ki-ya said—" began Bryna.

"Maybe Ki-ya's just dead!" spat Dart.

Bryna stood up, suddenly agitated. She licked furiously at the scabby stump of her tail.

There was a long moment's silence.

"*I* know a way," said Mr Edwards, unexpectedly, with an enthusiastic wag of his tail. "I says to myself, I says; we can live right under that silly bird's beak – day and night – and he won't even realise we're there."

Both Dart and Bryna were staring at Mr Edwards in disbelief. Maybe the mad old dog wasn't quite so mad after all.

"How?"

"Have you forgotten already why I'm here, missus? Come on – I'll show you."

"Show us?"

"Aye—! And I promise, there'll be a proper bed to sleep in and a decent meal to fill the emptiest of bellies."

"Pah! What is the crazy fool talking about?" spat Dart. "What are you going to do, take that silly bag of yours and go shopping for our supper?"

"Aye, well, maybe I am, maybe I am." Mr Edwards gave Bryna a knowing nudge. "It's time we did ourselves a spot of house-hunting." The mad dog was beginning to prove himself the most resourceful of them all.

"He's talking about getting inside the buildings, isn't he?" said Dart, still puzzled. "*Inside* the buildings?" The few houses the town cats and dogs had found open to them had long been stripped bare of anything useful, or remotely edible.

"Locks and handles," said Mr Edwards knowingly. And that was all he said by way of explanation.

"Sorry?" said Dart.

"Locks and handles," repeated Bryna, adding rather proudly, "Just think of him as our secret weapon!"

"Aye, well, I just hope Skrinkle doesn't get wind of our secret weapon. If he ever gets to think there's an endless supply of food and drink just sitting there, right under his nose, there'll be no stopping him. Locks and bolts are one thing. Bulls and wild animals are another! And hc won't be wanting the likes of you or me kept alive to stock up his larder!"

Their return journey to the town was long and slow. They were forced to travel at Dart's pace, and every step she took along the road made her wince, made her shudder with pain. It was simply good luck that they reached the outskirts of the town without misadventure, and just as the evening sun was sinking below the rooftops, masking their approach behind shadow.

Even with the gathering darkness they dared not walk openly on to the streets. There was a peculiar, disturbing lack of noise and movement. An impossible, eerie stillness that seemed capable of stopping the trees bending against the night's breeze. What was worse, it was not quiet because the streets were empty. No. More than once they ran into a cat sitting morosely by a garden gate, or a dog skulking in the deep shadows of a doorway. None spoke, not even to complain about their sudden appearance. They either slunk off into the night, or else simply sat where they were, fear-struck; looking blankly out into the darkness, waiting for the bird or the foxes to come for them. There was no helping them.

Mr Edwards kept them moving until they came upon a short row of red-bricked terraced houses, where he stopped, almost in recognition.

"What now?" whispered Dart.

"You'll see," said Bryna.

Dart watched in amazement as Mr Edwards used his paws to raise himself upright against the first front door in a neat line of front doors. There was a round brass handle that moved under the pressure of his jaws. Then the door swung open.

"Welcome home," said Mr Edwards cheerfully, disappearing inside.

"Do I have to, Bryna?" said Dart, a confirmed outsider by nature. (Though she was intrigued by the thought that any of these closed houses might mysteriously hold a secret store of food and water that could save all their lives.)

"Yes. Yes, you do," said Bryna, following after the dog, taking the reluctant Dart with her.

The house Mr Edwards had chosen was no different to any other house. It was simply Number One in the street. It still stank of men, even so long after their evacuation. There were four large rooms upstairs, three downstairs; and all stuffed full of useless human furniture. It was the kitchen that took Mr Edwards' attention. Though he rather enjoyed showing off his secret talent for opening closed doors (and closing open doors, of course; which worried Dart sick).

Unfortunately, Number One wasn't a spectacular success. The kitchen cupboards were empty of food, and try as he might, he could not open any of the water taps enough to give them a drink.

"This house-hunting lark isn't really all it's cracked up to be, is it?" grumbled Dart.

Mr Edwards pretended he hadn't heard. He opened up the front door of Number One again, and led them the few short paces to Number Two. The front door was locked shut, with no handle to grasp; and no amount of cursing, pushing or shoving made the slightest difference. Number Three had a proper handle but it too was locked. So was Number Four.

"How much longer do we keep this up?" asked Dart, anxiously.

"Until we find another door that does open, of course," said Bryna.

The door to Number Five was already standing open. Mr Edwards took it upon himself to explore the inside alone; just in case there was some animal at home who needed persuading of their good intent. The door had obviously been open for a very long time. The hall was badly weather-stained and it stank of stale urine. Most of the rooms stood bare, except for a few threads of carpet, and had been slept in at some time by both cats and dogs. And there was the more recent wild scent of another animal he did not recognise.

And then, at last, Mr Edwards struck lucky. The very next front door, Number Six, opened easily, with a long handle that needed only the weight of one front paw to move it. Directly behind the door a large metal chair was barring their way, but because it had been built conveniently on wheels it was easily pushed aside. Inside, most of the room doors had been wedged permanently open.

Better still, in the kitchen the cupboards were fitted at such a low height Mr Edwards could easily reach the top shelves without having to climb up on to the worktops; *and* they were all stuffed full of packets and jars, tins and bottles. But best of all, the house had never been touched by a single strange paw. Everything was intact. It was almost as if their visit had been planned for. Even the water tap in the kitchen sink had a special long handle that needed only the slightest touch of a nose to let the water out.

To Bryna's delight, Mr Edwards announced, with a great flourish of his wagging tail, that he had indeed found them a bed for the night. "Couldn't have made it better if I'd built it for myself," he said.

Then he pushed the front door closed with his nose. Shut them all inside.

"I hope this mad dog knows what he's doing," Dart hissed under her breath. "Doesn't go and die on us while we're stuck in here . . ." She slumped to the floor, suddenly exhausted, little more than a shadow among the dark shadows of the room that surrounded her.

Nineteen

Howlers and Looters

It was always going to be Dart who found it most difficult to stay shut inside a house, behind closed doors. It was not in her nature, and even cruelly injured as she was, she did not, could not settle to it. (No matter how often Mr Edwards or Bryna tried persuading her otherwise.) Then again, what choice was there but to stay well hidden? As yet they had no plan of action.

By day they turned their ears and noses to the outside world and listened to the pattern of the town. Skrinkle's mark was everywhere. How often they heard the shriek of the warrior bird as he flew over the town warning unwary animals, if there could be such animals, of his presence. How often they heard the scrat-a-pat of paws against the pavements outside, as small bands of foxes marched by; periodically howling in praise of their beloved leader. And then the feeble-voiced replies: the pitiful cries of dogs and cats, mimicking the call of the foxes. Hoping for a scrap of meat; hoping to avoid the cut of a claw.

It was only under the cover of night that Mr Edwards, Bryna and Dart felt brave enough to attempt a serious prowl about the town. And always with dead Grundle walking secretly with them in the shadows. Keeping them out of harm's way. Ensuring they avoided any fox or bird, bull or other strange creature that might be lurking in the darkness.

Night after night, they prowled that way, gradually building up a pattern of the doors that were open to them. And there was always a wild, strangely wondrous look about Mr

Edwards when they returned home. Indeed, Bryna had never known him so enthusiastic, so illuminated and certain of himself (not even before Sugar's fake death).

"Do you know just how many doors there are in *one* street, Bryna? Eh, Dart? Do you know how many streets there are in a whole town? We're spoilt for choice. Spoilt for choice! And shops, shops—! I know you told me, Bryna. I know you explained, but I never imagined, couldn't imagine, not in my wildest dreams! And I says to myself, I says, where there's shops to be had there's food to be had. And where there's houses there's water to drink and places to hide . . ."

And if all of the huge department stores were firmly locked and bolted, shuttered with steel guards and impenetrable, many of the small corner shops and most of the houses had simply had their doors pulled closed on that night, long ago, when men abandoned them. They had stayed that way ever since – shut but not locked – just waiting for a dog with the knack to come and open them up again.

And all the while, the town cats and dogs stayed well out of their way: untrusting, and untrustworthy. It seemed they came in only the two sorts.

There were those in thrall to Skrinkle-the-fox, who hankered blindly after him, and refused to see anything peculiar in the disappearance of close kin; even as murder was done.

And there were those who *did* see, who *did* understand Skrinkle's methods, but were too scared, too struck with fear, too far beyond hope to do anything about it.

One night they stumbled across a frail, sickening tom cat, caught asleep in the shadows of a doorway. "Stay, my friend, stay. I will not harm you," said Dart, her voice soft and gentle. "We can give you food and water to drink and—"

Instantly, the ailing tom cat found strength enough to move, and he scuttled off into the night to die alone.

"How can we possibly help animals who will not *be* helped! Who will not even listen to our words?" spat Dart. "How can we hope to rid the town of Skrinkle's evil when it is already as good as lost to him?"

And so it was.

"At least with Mr Edwards' talent for house-breaking *we* can always hide in safety," said Bryna. "What fox, what bird or any other animal for that matter, is going to think of looking for cats and dogs *behind* a closed front door?"

"Aye – true enough. But in the end, where does that get us?" said Dart. "How are we ever going to bring Skrinkle and men face to face, let alone make them fight, if all we can do is hide?"

It was a question without an answer. There didn't seem to be a way of doing it. Dead

Grundle stood quietly in the shadows, shaking his head.

And then, early one evening, some animal came scratching at their front door.

Mr Edwards and Dart exchanged a look that was undisguised horror. "What animal can that be?" hissed Dart, opening her claws. She was still in a sorry state – if better fed, now – but she would stand and fight at Bryna's side if she had to.

Bryna sat bolt upright, ears alert.

The scratching came again, and with it an urgent muffled voice. "Open up this door will you — Before some prowling gang of foxes sees us standing here!"

Mr Edwards and the two cats stayed silent.

"Oh, come on, Bryna! We know you're in there," continued the first muffled voice. "We were certain you were all dead; until we heard the rumours of your return."

"Maybe's that's all they were, rumours," said a second muffled voice, sadly . . .

"They know your name—" hissed Dart.

"Shhhh . . ."

"Bryna, listen! It's me. It's *me*, Kim. Kim and there's Sleekit here with me!"

"Kim *and* Sleekit?" cried Dart and Bryna together. Both cats were standing now, tails upright and agitated, pawing the hall carpet behind the front door.

Mr Edwards stood upon his hind legs and opened the door. Two desperate, bedraggled animals fell into the hall.

There was no jubilant welcome as old friends and kin met. Kim and Sleekit, Bryna and Dart each spoke in turn, but could only tell as much of their stories as their heavy hearts would allow. It was enough that, beyond all hope, they had found each other alive. There would be time enough to ask deeper questions, to wonder, to mourn lost friends, to celebrate, when the town was rid of fox and vixen, bird and bull.

"... So, so you're telling me, Ki-ya's ghost told Bryna to bring the green metal men and the foxes *together*?" said Kim, trying to get the idea right in his head while he finished off a second plate of food miraculously provided by the strange Mr Edwards from his kitchen.

"How – how *exactly* are you going to do that, then?" asked Sleekit.

Bryna and Dart sat vacantly.

"We don't know," said Mr Edwards, looking sadly down into his own empty dinner plate. "We just don't know."

"It would be no use trying to lure Skrinkle to the soldiers. He's too quick, too sly to be led so easily into a trap. And besides, there's all his cronies!" said Bryna, thoughtfully. "So that means bringing the soldiers into the town. Bringing them to him. But I don't know how it could be done ..."

* * *

The answer to their problem came out of the blue, and from a most unexpected source. Early one evening, Mr Edwards was outside, prowling with Kim and Sleekit (who had learnt to walk the streets as secretly as any ghost). It was then that it happened. They were caught unawares between front doors, by a noise that stopped them in their tracks. Indeed, every animal across the town who heard it, and that was most, stood still and worry-struck. It wasn't a sudden noise. Now that it was loud enough to scare them, Kim realised it had been there a long time, gradually increasing in volume. Not an animal noise. Something mechanical.

The roar of engines. The engines of metal road machines. Getting louder. Coming nearer.

Together dogs and cat pricked their ears, determined to understand. And as they did they heard the distant cry of the warrior bird frantically squealing his alarm across the evening sky as he flew for home.

Inside Skrinkle's den, as the noises grew, they echoed across the walls, and seemed more dreadful than they really were. In the dark of the church, foxes began pacing nervously backwards and forwards, or else slunk back against its walls as if the weight of the stones would afford them some kind of protection. And though they were huddled safely together against their mother, Slivid's cubs began to cry out, to wet themselves with fear.

Outside, Mr Edwards, Kim and Sleekit cowered in the street, not sure whether to be more afraid of the noises or the agitated bird.

As the roar of the engines grew even louder the reality began to sink in. If it *was* metal road machines, if they *were* moving about the streets, then that could mean only one thing . . .

"There'll be men!" said Sleekit. "Men in the town!"

"Aye . . ." said Kim. "And soldiers—!"

Far away, squealing with contempt, Skrinkle-the-bird withdrew deep into the heart of his church den; plummeted into the safe darkness of his tower, felt himself become fox again almost before he touched the ground. For all his noise and bluster, for the very first time ever, there was a hesitant edge to his call. And his smell had changed.

Fear.

He was scared. Skrinkle-the-fox could be frightened after all. And it was men, even the very thought of men, that frightened him most.

All of a sudden the noises out on the street stopped. The engines had been switched off.

"Come on," said Mr Edwards, excitedly. "I must see this!"

"You daft beggar!" growled Kim. "If it is machines, then it's *men*!"

"Yes! Isn't it wonderful?" The mad dog was already moving again. Kim looked at Sleekit for support, but the cat could only lick at his patched fur.

"Oh, all right, we're coming. But if you get us all killed, don't blame me."

When they found the metal road machines, they were part of a scene that, at first, did not make sense. There was a pair of lorries slewed awkwardly across the road, brought to a stop in a careless hurry. Their rear doors stood gaping wide, like giant hungry mouths, and they were being fed with a strange meal of white metal boxes. At least, that was how it appeared to the dogs and the cat. There was a large group of men, running backwards and forwards between the lorries and the shop buildings. Constantly to-ing and fro-ing. Carrying and lifting. And they were being deliberately noisy, banging about, randomly smashing plate glass windows with an uneasy mock bravado, as if they were challenging the empty street to fight them back.

These lorries were not soldiers' lorries – too big, too square, too *red.* And each had the huge picture of a grinning man painted on its sides; making the lorries look as if they were very, very pleased with themselves. And these men on the street were not the green metal men. No bucket-sized metal heads, no long iron sticks or uniforms. No order or discipline. And they smelled anxious, furtive, scared even.

Kim watched their antics only with a feeling of hollow emptiness . . . No love, or hate. No excitement, or fear. For Kim, men simply no longer belonged in the town. They were out of place there. Alien. Though only Mr Edwards understood exactly what it was he saw . . . Thieves. Looters.

Both dogs suddenly wanted these men

gone. Felt their hackles rise and deep, warning growls lifting in their throats.

"Hey, steady on there. Steady—!" hissed Sleekit. But he stood his ground with the dogs all the same.

Then the men saw them.

There had been a constant irritable bickering, thin nervous laughter and foul curses spat backwards and forwards between the men, as if they were each their own worst enemies. Now they spat their curses at the animals, thankful of the distraction. Laughing out loud at the same time, as if it was all some huge joke.

"What's them mangy old beggars up to then, Duggy?"

"They've prob'ly got the rabies or summat. Aye, they'll be as mad as sin. Prob'ly come to get you, Nobby old son!" Still the men laughed.

"Aye, well, I'll soon fix them — Bugger off the lot of you—!" yelled the man called

Nobby. "Go on with yer—!" In his arms he was carrying a big white metal box, with knobs and switches and trailing wires; and a metal door left flapping carelessly open and shut. Without a thought he lifted it above his head and hurled it at Kim. The white box landed with a bouncing crash, skittering across the road like a demented metal animal, spitting bits of itself at Kim as it came. Luckily, it did not travel far and stopped well short.

"Who's the mad beggar now then, Nobby? That stuff's worth a packet."

"Plenty more where that'n come from—" said Nobby. "I told you lot this town was a bloody gold mine. Should have been here months ago. And anyway, them animals is givin' me the willies. They're looking at me funny."

"Aw, come on, don't be so daft. Let's just get on with the job and get out of this stinking place. It's not cats and dogs you've got to worry about, it's those bloody border guards – if they ever decide to take a look this way, you'll know about it."

The men started back towards the shops, still laughing, only to stop again suddenly and exchange an odd look.

Kim cocked his head; there was a new noise. A distant mechanical fwump, fwump, fwump.

The men stopped laughing.

"Here, what the heck's that? You had to open your big mouth, Duggy, didn't you? Now all of you, shut your rotten faces and listen!"

Suddenly, there it was, hovering just above the rooftops like some awful giant insect. Its noise was deafening. Its huge metal wings twirled above its bulbous one-eyed head, chopping the still air into an instant whirlwind; throwing loose debris across the street. It pushed the looters off their feet as, in their panic, they rushed to hide inside the shops. Pushed Mr Edwards, Kim and Sleekit too: lifted them, rolled them easily aside.

Then, without warning, came the shriek. An impossible angry squeal that was louder even than the roar of the engine. A foul sound that some instinct warned Kim of death. Death. Ugly and terrible.

In the next moment he was dropped suddenly into some doorway. He did not hear the sound of the explosion. That was all the time it took.

The big red lorries with the smiling faces were gone. The men, Nobby and Duggy among them, were gone. The shopfronts, even the road they had all been standing on, were gone. In their place a savage, gaping hole. It was as if the flying giant had taken a huge bite out of the street.

The thudding of the helicopter's rotor blades faded away gently as it disappeared over the rooftops and back across the border fence to the north, from where it had come to seek out the intruders.

"Come on, Sleekit, I think it's over," said Kim, cautiously. "And time we weren't here."

"I don't think I can move," said Sleekit. "I think I'm dead."

"You'll be dead in a minute, if that Skrinkle plucks up the courage to come and take a nosey this way," said Mr Edwards.

Unchallenged, the three animals edged their way silently out of the street, lost themselves in the growing darkness.

There was not a single animal in that town who was not affected by the intrusion of the looters and their sudden, violent deaths. For the rest of that night and most of the next day there was no movement on the streets. Not on the ground. Not in the air.

Inside the terraced house, at Number Six, it was the same; dogs and cats stayed put, anxious and disturbed. None of them sure what to make of it all.

None of them, except Mr Edwards that is . . .

The longer he spent thinking about the looters, thinking about the fwump fwump fwump of the awful metal flying machine, thinking about the dreadful power of its sting, the more certain he became. In the end, he couldn't stop himself from pacing excitedly up and down, or his tail from wagging furiously, which only served to unnerve his companions even more.

"What is the matter with that loony dog?" Dart hissed at Sleekit. "Hasn't he had enough excitement for one lifetime?" At first Mr Edwards didn't seem to notice Dart's questions, and no other animal was in the mood to answer. And then the dog suddenly stood still and barked his announcement.

"I've got it!"

"Got it? Got what?" asked Bryna, curious.

"I knew there was an answer there somewhere."

"Answer to what?"

"To bringing men and foxes face to face, of course."

"Ye-s—?" said Kim, sitting up attentively.

"Don't you see? We now know there is *one* thing that's guaranteed to lure the green metal men into the town."

"Do we?" asked Dart. "And what's that, then?"

"Other men," said Mr Edwards.

"Other men?"

"Isn't that exactly what we witnessed with our own eyes, Sleekit?"

"Well, yes, yes, I suppose so . . ." said Sleekit a little doubtfully. "But where's the good in it? There aren't any other men in the town to lure anybody anywhere. So . . . so I don't really see how that helps us."

"It might," said Mr Edwards, excitedly beating his tail. "I can't rustle you up any real live men. Not skin and bone. But I says to myself, I says; I might just be able to make the town *look* as if there's men here."

"How?" asked Sleekit.

"Wheels," he said. "Wheels and hand-brakes. Aye, and maybe even engines too!"

"Eh—?" Dart and Sleekit exchanged quizzical glances, nudged Bryna for help, certain that Mr Edwards really was barking mad. Bryna only began to purr, as she remembered her late afternoon strolls with the dog around Fenholm, and their "drives" together in his car.

"You know, if any animal could do it, it would be Mr Edwards," said Bryna, suddenly excited. "And now that we're talking illusions; to help things along a bit we could set us a whole army against that fox in his den. At least give him and his cronies something else to think about!"

"We haven't got an army! Have we?" said

Kim, worried now that Bryna had somehow caught Mr Edwards' madness.

"Yes, we have," said Bryna, "There's my ghosts!"

"Oh, I see. Ghosts again," said Dart without enthusiasm. She never had been one for ghosts.

Twenty

The Beacon

There followed a curious time, with Mr Edwards forever slipping out on to the streets in the dead of the night. Always with blind Bryna for company. And always with dead Grundle watching out for them; keeping them safe.

And when they returned home they came full of mad talk: about engines and hand brakes, sloping streets, gears and steering wheels. None of it made a jot of sense to the animals they had left behind.

"I says to myself, I says; never you mind, though. Rest yourselves. Save your strength. We'll all of us have our parts to play before this thing is done with."

Almost every street in the town had its abandoned metal road machine. Cars and lorries mostly; so long ago left for dead at the side of the roads by fleeing men. They had been of little use to starving dogs and cats – except perhaps as temporary shelter – and so, by and large, had been ignored. Mr Edwards studied every one of them in turn. And though they all excited him wildly, none of them seemed to be *just* what he was looking for. Not *quite* big enough. Not in *quite* the right place. He was not satisfied, could not be satisfied – against Bryna's better judgement – until he was close, dangerously close, to Skrinkle's own den.

They found themselves high up the valley side, and on a steep slope, looking down into a shadowy darkness; to where Skrinkle's church tower and the mass of his hordes lay hidden before them.

Dead Grundle had looked worried then, his bird cack-cackered furiously, desperate for them to move safely away. But Mr Edwards had found something there, something important. It was a bus. A huge double-decker; slewed across the pavement where it had been abandoned; its doors left open to the elements. (Soon after Skrinkle's arrival in the town the foxes had set a guard there; but not for long. What was the point? What was there to guard against?)

"One man's rubbish is another man's treasure," whispered Mr Edwards, excitedly.

There was to be one last discovery. And in the event an even greater find, though it came about by accident when Mr Edwards found his way into the basement of a tall department store. It stood not on Skrinkle's street, but close by, and in sight of it. Indeed, near enough to the top of the hill to overlook the whole river valley. "*And* with its own generator, missus! Its own generator! And you know what that means?"

"No," said Bryna, flatly. "No, I don't."

"Lights!"

"Lights?" Bryna looked quizzically at the dog.

"Yes, electric lights – that will shine like a beacon out into the world," Mr Edwards was howling with excitement. "And if that doesn't worry your fox, doesn't get your green metal men interested, *nothing* will!"

Little else could be done in preparation. There could be no dress rehearsal. Only the doing.

Twenty-One

THE ARMY THAT NEVER WAS

"Will they come?" asked Dart, poking her nose out of the front door of Number Six, before moving cautiously on to the street. "Those ghosts of yours, will they come for us?"

"Yes," said Bryna, following after her, certain of herself. "I have called them. They will *all* come. They will show themselves." Dead Grundle and Ki-ya had promised her. And inside her head, she had called out again and again; cried the name of every animal she had ever known, any name she could remember.

Dart looked nervously about her, wondering if one or two phantoms were perhaps already there. It was late afternoon.

The naked sun stood low upon the horizon, but the streets of the town were still blindingly bright, and hot enough for the pavements to sting their paws as they walked. The air around them tumbled in restless heat flurries against the walls of buildings. No cooling evening breeze. No darkness to shade them yet.

They had deliberately chosen this part of the day to set out. Mr Edwards had insisted.

"When your antics on the streets begin they must be obvious to draw the attention of the fox. Because I'll be already out there, and on my own this time. I says to myself, I says; if Skrinkle's looking at you, he isn't looking at me! And it's all about timing. As the dusk falls – click!"

"Click?"

"Aye, missus. Click. And the lights of the town will shine again. And your green metal men watching from their tall towers upon the Outland hills will see for certain. And, curious, they will come looking."

"Aye – but can you make it work?" Dart had asked. "If your plan goes untested, how do you know it will work?"

"I don't," said Mr Edwards. And that was all he said.

So, there they were, blind Bryna and Dart. With Kim and Sleekit soon following after them.

It was not an impressive sight. Not much of an army on the march.

"Where are you lot off to, then?" asked some cat in hiding, suddenly curious as they moved his way.

"Off to do battle with Skrinkle, of course," Dart called back, honestly enough, though unsure of where the cat-call had come from. "Will you fight with us, friend?"

"Pah! I think that bird took off more than your fur when he burned you up in his fire." The cat fell silent and wasn't heard again.

They marched on. Kept stubbornly to the middle of the empty streets. Moved slowly towards the fox's den.

And then, quite unexpectedly, they came . . .

Bryna's ghosts.

No obvious movement. No change in the silent day. No shadow fallen across the sun. The first was Grundle, suddenly there with his sparrow sitting on his shoulder, walking quietly at Bryna's side. And then came Ki-ya following after his sister Dart (if only she had known it).

Then, to Kim's left, walked the greyhound, Cherry, her tail whipping with excitement. Bryna's head began to feel heavy and dull with the weight of their numbers. And more and more came with every step. There was the Labrador, Fisher, with her young dog-pup, Saal, bravely marching with them. Ghosts in front of them now. Ghosts behind them, in a growing line that threaded back through the streets and twisted out of sight. And still they came, numbers beyond counting, dogs and cats named and unnamed. Toms and queens. Moggies and mongrels. Lap-cats and strays. The dead of a thousand generations.

Soon even living animals could not fail to see them there. If only as whispering shadows fallen across the town where no shadows had a business to be.

Upon his rooftop perch, Skrinkle-the-bird saw them too. So many shadows, so many strange shapes folding and unfolding, puzzling his eyes as they moved through the streets. He slipped quietly from his perch and lifted himself into the sky. Far below him the shadows were spreading. Cats and dogs, there, not there. Sometimes solid, sometimes less than a trail of smoke from the embers of a grassland fire.

But surely, there was blood and bone there too? A handful of *real* cats and dogs among these shifting ghosts?

In silence, Skrinkle-the-bird turned upon the air, folded back his wings and slipped from the sky like a breath of wind. There was no time for any animal to flee before him. None saw his coming until it was too late—

Until his talons struck, and he lifted his victim off its paws.

"Stand your ground," cried Bryna, suddenly aware – even in her blindness – of what was happening. "Stand your ground, and keep moving."

And Dart cried with her. "We must not falter, not now!"

"But the bird has taken Sleekit!" snarled Kim, snapping his jaws uselessly at the empty air where the warrior bird had come and gone. "He's taken your *own* son!"

Dart mewed in anguish, driving her claws

deep into the warm tar of the road, determined to stand firm. "He has what he wants — Keep on!"

Skrinkle's brutal talons dug deep into Sleekit's poor frail body. The pain – shrill and piercing – seemed to fill his whole self. In that one moment he knew for certain that he must die. And yet . . . and yet somehow it did not worry him. Not the pain. Not the beat of the great warrior bird's wings, or the world spinning around and around far below him. It was almost like a dream, a beautiful hazy dream. And there he was flying. Flying on top of the world.

Skrinkle-the-bird began to screech questions at him, digging his talons even deeper as if to squeeze the answers out of him. "Speak, rancid flea-bag. Speak! Before I turn your guts free upon the wind. What *is* all this? What *is* all this?"

Sleekit dreamt on. He did not mind pretending to struggle against the bird, and when he could take the pain no longer he knew there was no shame in answering truthfully.

"Go and tell your master . . . go and tell him that his life is forfeit, that his reign of terror is over, and yours with it. Go and tell him that Bryna's army has come for him!"

And so, Sleekit spoke his last and died.

His final words, his strange prophecy, concerned the bird. But surely the cat had not known his secret?

"Ka—!" Skrinkle-the-bird opened his talons and dropped the carcass, watched it fall, watched it break against the dry bed of the river and lie still.

He set his wings against the rising wind and turned himself towards his church tower.

Twenty-Two

The Battle that Never was

The huge wooden door of the church had been flung wide open. And there, standing alone in the doorway, was the vixen, Slivid. Far above her, Skrinkle-the-bird was perched quietly on the church tower. Unworried, he did not stir; not even as Bryna began to march her strange army of ghosts past the stricken metal body of the bus, and into the street from the top of the hill.

"What is it that you want, my friends?" cried Slivid, proudly defiant. "What is it that brings you together in such great numbers?"

"You do!" barked Kim. "You and all of your bloody kin!"

"Aye, and where is your master, now?" spat Dart. "Scared of a few poor pussies, is he?"

"Is that a threat, my friends?" Slivid cast a knowing eye towards Skrinkle's tower. The bird gave an impressive, piercing squeal that echoed across the street, and had living cats and dogs cowering against the ground. But not enough to stop their advance.

Blind Bryna walked on, following dead Grundle, with Dart walking nervously at her side.

"Tell me again, Bryna, there *is* a whole army marching with us, isn't there?" she hissed. "You're not just making it up? We're not just a handful of silly fools?"

"Heed our warning," cried Slivid. "Stay your ground. Stay, I say." Suddenly there were foxes streaming through the church doorway, surrounding her. It was a deliberate, planned show of strength.

But then again, to cats and dogs it was also something of a puzzle. A few foxes? A single bird of prey? Where were the other foul beasts that made up their numbers?

Bryna began to purr. "Yes, we have a whole army, Dart, a whole army. And your own brother stands with us."

"Eh?"

A slight breeze caught a piece of litter and rattled it across the street, and with it came a voice that seemed to whisper to her. "There is time for just one last hunt together, my sister. One last kill. Let's make it a good one."

Suddenly they were all running at once. Dogs and cats, alive and dead, charging towards the foxes.

"Kill them!" shrieked Slivid, full of bluster as they came on. "Kill every one of them. Stain the streets with their stinking blood. A mark of warning to any creature foolish enough to threaten *my* master!"

"Oh, charming!" growled Kim.

* * *

It was a blunt, uncontrolled attack. But to Skrinkle-the-bird the charge looked impressive, dangerous even. And below him, on the ground, Slivid was not as confident as she sounded. The street was full to bursting with angry cats and dogs, and they were all charging towards *his* church.

The warrior bird stayed put. Held his ground.

It was only a pity that the best part of Bryna's army were ghosts. Because, when it came down to it, they weren't much good at fighting with ordinary flesh and blood. The ghosts looked spectacular, with snarling teeth and flashing claws, but they had an unfortunate habit of running straight *through* their enemies, dissolving away into nothingness as they made their attacks.

At first it was confusing for the foxes to discover an enemy that could not be bitten, that did not bite back. And even more disconcerting to find one or two among them that did! But the advantage of surprise was soon gone.

Still Skrinkle-the-bird stood fast upon his tower, biding his time.

The few living dogs and cats did what damage they could. Had a go at any piece of fox that got in their way. Tried not to stand still in one place too long. Bryna simply followed dead Grundle into the battle. Shadowed his every move, struck out wherever she thought it might help.

Dart quickly found herself on the stone steps of the church, face to face with Slivid, and took a swipe at the vixen's snout. Drew blood there.

But where on earth was Mr Edwards? Where was the mad dog with his beacon, his wheels and his engines? Where were the green metal men he was supposed to be bringing to defeat the foxes?

It was not the mad dog, not men either, that came down upon them then.

It was Skrinkle.

Skrinkle-the-bird fell out of the sky like a dropped stone. In one motion his talons cut into poor Dart's flesh, and tossed the cat carelessly aside without bothering to finish her off.

Then, for one brief instant, the bird became the fox again, standing anxiously at his mate's side. But the next there was a bull stomping and pounding, angrily grinding its hooves against the ground. Then a snake spitting poison. Then a huge brown bear, that took the wind out of Kim with a single sideways swipe of its powerful arm. Then, bird again squealing its contempt. So quickly did Skrinkle move between one shape and the next it was almost impossible to set the animals apart.

And so, Skrinkle's strange secret was at last revealed. There was no army of wild Outland creatures. Just as there was no army of dogs and cats; only fleeting ghosts.

Skrinkle's beasts were all one and the same animal.

All one and the same animal.

Could it be so? There was no time to puzzle it out. The truth did not lessen the strength of Skrinkle's sudden attack.

Momentarily, Dart and Kim, both injured, found themselves side by side, backing away from the vicious onslaught. Luckily, Bryna was close enough to sense their movement. All at once they were retreating back up the hill with Skrinkle-the-bear, Slivid and foxes charging after them; blood up, drunk with the excitement of the battle.

And then, at last – at long, long last there was Mr Edwards.

"Look! Look—! *Inside* the bus—!" cried Kim with sudden joy. The mad dog was sitting in the driver's seat, excitedly working his jaws against the steering wheel, tugging and pulling at the knobs and levers that surely must make the machine go.

The huge body of the double-decker rocked unsteadily backwards and forwards, shuddered and groaned, only to fall still and silent. But then, quite suddenly, it moved again, gave a lurch; its axles squealing above the noise of the battle.

Startled, tiring quickly from his constant, foolish and frantic transformations, Skrinkle-the-bear did not have time to get out of the way of the bus as it began to roll down the hill. He took the first blow head on. Any lesser animal would have been killed outright, but not him. He fell to the ground stunned, only to stagger upright again. Slivid came instantly to him, howling encouragement, persuading him once more to the attack.

Kim launched himself, at last understanding the cruel trick Skrinkle had played upon them all this time; planted his teeth upon an open wound at the bear's throat. But still there was no killing done. Yet again,

Skrinkle-the-bird took shape, striking out with beak and talon, wildly beating his wings until he struggled free and flew high above the rooftops of the town.

Beneath him, the squealing bus rolled on. Picking up speed, with Mr Edwards struggling for control at the steering wheel. He must have turned it to the left because the bus scraped across the kerb on that side of the street and ran along the face of the buildings, bouncing angrily as it went. Luckily the hill was steep and the impact wasn't enough to stop its forward motion.

The bus kept on rolling.

Whose side the bus was on, even with Mr Edwards behind the wheel, wasn't very clear. It rolled towards dogs and cats, foxes and fading ghosts with the same detached, eager relish.

Then it hit the first abandoned car. Mr Edwards gave up his struggle and let go of the steering wheel, used his whole body weight to hurl himself out through the open passenger door. On its own now, the bus lurched back into the middle of the road pushing the empty car before it.

The car ran off down the hill, caught a glancing blow against a second car and ran them both through the plate glass of a large shop window.

Out of control, the bus was still moving at great speed and did not stop, not even when it reached the steps of the church. It seemed to scramble up them. Simply pushed the great wooden door out of its way, taking half of the face of the building with it; before finally coming to an uneasy rest among the debris, its back wheels spinning off the ground.

From the sky, Skrinkle-the-bird watched in anger as the tail-end of the battle unfolded below him. Panicking foxes, chasing after the bus as it ran up the church steps.

In the growing dusk he saw Mr Edwards scuttling off up the street, away from the wreckage. Watched, as miraculously the dog stood upon his hind legs, opened a door and disappeared *inside* a building close by.

And as he watched, he began to understand enough of what he saw to worry. Surely, it looked for all the world as if men had returned to the town; what with the weight of dust, blown up by fighting animals, and the cars and the bus rolling about in the middle of the street.

Could there have been a plan in it? Could it all have been deliberate?

He wheeled himself about, flew higher and higher. Turned his eye upon the Outland hills, upon the border fences to the north and to the south that stretched out like a pair of endless ruled lines between horizons; and upon the watch towers where men's eyes in their turn looked forever back towards him. Did they see it all? Did they know? Did they understand?

And then a light shone. Sudden, immediate, blindingly bright. A single scratch of artificial light that came from inside the town, that cut the sky in two and shone out like a great beacon, more brilliant now than the fading sun. It was there, and then it was gone. Off and then on again. Off and then on. Giving a simple message that could not be misunderstood. Look at me, *look at me,* I am here.

Far away, in the small dark prison that was their wooden crate, Treacle and Lugger heard the commotion; the soldiers arguing among themselves at the door of the storeroom.

"You can't take them cats up the ruddy watch tower!"

"Why ever not—? They're my regimental mascots."

"Mascots, my backside! Just don't let Sarge see them, that's all—"

Then the cats felt the sudden movement of the crate as it was roughly lifted, carried outside and up the ringing iron steps of the watch tower. Felt too a sting of pain as the last of the fading daylight zigzagged between the wooden slats and caught their eyes; too long cooped up in the dark.

The crate was set down and soon there was more jibber-jabber from the soldiers. Swearing and name-calling, but this time all said in such low, settled voices it was obviously just a game, and idle banter. Until, shocked, Smithie suddenly yelled out—

"Bloody hell, Jock. Something down there just moved."

"Where? Give me those binoculars!"

"There! *There!* In the town, where do you think? It was a bus. A bright red bus; and it moved!"

"What bus? I can't see a bus! I think this

heat's finally getting to you, old son. First you bring that daft crate of cats up the tower, and now you're seeing shadows in the dusk!"

When his eyes stopped hurting, Treacle, intrigued, tried to look out between the wooden slats of the crate. A little bit of blue sky. Something green. Something grey. Some distant shape, vague and hazy. Nothing much.

"Well, of course you can't see a bus *now,* because it's not there *now,* is it?" said Smithie. "It'll be halfway down the hill, heading for the river."

"Barmy so and so!"

"No, I'm not — just you keep watching. The streets twist our way as they move down the valley. You'll see — There! What the heck's that if it's not a bus? *And* cars! Ruddy well cars too, moving about! They're kicking up enough dust! What the heck's going on?"

"Looters," yelled Jock. "Looters again, it's got to be."

"You'd think they'd learn their lesson, wouldn't you—? After that helicopter gunship went in and did for the last lot of the daft beggars. Never even stopped to pick up the bits!"

"Aye, well, that's the way that lot north of the border work, isn't it? It's a sin. There's no messin' about with slapped wrists. Straight in with the heavies and goodnight sweetheart!"

"Aye, and a lot of good it did them! Nearly started another war. Politicians getting on their high horses again, demanding retaliation. Everybody heaping the blame on to everybody else."

"Well, you know the orders, same as me. Between them border wires – north *and* south – is a bloody no-man's-land. That means nobody don't go into it. Nobody don't come out of it. At least, not alive. And if there's policing to be done our lot of stuffed shirts want *us* to be the ones to do it. And a proper example set this time."

"Come on, we'd better get on to him who must be obeyed."

"Aye, aye, or – or maybe we could just leave old Sarge in blissful ignorance for once. You know, if we're quick about it, we could get ourselves a truck, be in the town and away again before anybody noticed. Unofficial, like. Get the silly beggars out before they get themselves flattened."

"A truck on our own? You kiddin', Smithie? What if we were caught? That'd be us on a charge. And t'other side accusin' our side of starting a bloody invasion into the bargain!"

"Aye, well, let's leave all that stuff to the politicians, eh—?"

Suddenly, out of the falling dusk a streak of artificial light shone out from the town. Mr Edwards' light. On. Off. On again. Off again.

No more talk.

Treacle felt their box lifted and thrown across a shoulder, heard the clang clang clang of boots driven hard down the iron steps of the watch tower—

No animal, no bird quite understood the rapid sequence of events that was to follow. But Bryna remembered the smell ever afterwards. A strong pungent odour that stung her nose, that filled her mouth and throat with its foul fumes all at the same time.

The bus hadn't quite come to rest upon the collapsed church walls, and as its windows popped, its twisted metal raked and ground against the stonework, sending out tiny showers of needle-like sparks. And there was a liquid spilling out beneath the bus, almost as if it was bleeding to death.

Then came the first explosion, that wrapped the stricken double-decker inside a curtain of blue flame. How easily the church began to burn then. Its wooden door. Its wooden rafters and cladded walls. How very easily it began to burn.

The battle was not yet done.

Mr Edwards' electric lights blinked on and off as, deep inside his department store, he worked his jaws against the levers that brought his beloved generator roaring into life, that killed it stone dead again in an instant.

Skrinkle-the-bird wheeled across the sky, crying out in anger. Worried by the flashing lights; worried by the squealing blue flames that engulfed the bus. Unsure of how he could fight either. Inside his church his own cubs lay hidden still. Safely out of harm's way, he had thought.

Then, on the ground, there was Slivid his mate, yowling up at him in desperation, squealing for the lives of their cubs; the battle suddenly forgotten.

No animal could have stopped her as

she threw herself up the stone steps of the church and into the advancing flames. If she moved fast enough maybe she could outrun the fire; maybe she could save their young yet.

For the very last time Skrinkle-the-bird folded back his great wings and swooped out of the sky. He made his landing too hard; hit the church tower with such force the impact broke his wing. He did not care, took little notice; clambered his way inside the church tower, disappeared into its darkness.

Then, unseen, the men came.

From the south a sluggish trail of dust behind a single green lorry on an empty road.

From the north the flash of something silver-blue – first one, then two – both moving so rapidly against the deeper blue of the sky they could only be traced by the keenest of eyes. And the noise! No lazy helicopter's fwump fwump fwump this time, but a roaring fury, louder than any bolt of thunder, that drowned out all other sound and bloodied the ear. There had been great iron-winged birds in the sky before. But never a pair so angry. Never a pair so close to the ground; so quickly come, so quickly gone again. They passed by a second time. And then a third. And finally, their eyes had seen enough; had made up their own story from the scenes played out on the ground below them.

They came again, just once; each in turn to spit out its killing sting. And then no more.

The first missile struck the church. The second missile silenced Mr Edwards' generator for ever.

Those at the heart of the explosions were perhaps the lucky ones. They knew nothing about it, because it killed them outright.

Flame. Searing flame. Belching waves of scorched air. Tiny droplets of liquid metal falling like rain. Had the sun suddenly fallen out of the sky? Had it risen again amidst the buildings of the town to devour them all with its impossible heat, to blind them all with its impossible light? And an after-noise that did not seem to match the ugliness of the event somehow. A low regular beat – like a drum – reverberating through the streets; repeating itself in distant echoes across the town.

Skrinkle-the-fox and Slivid, caught together inside their fiery den, now *almost* within reach of their squealing cubs, could never have understood. The agony of their deaths – and so many with them – was such a terrible thing it is right that we do not look too closely there.

Out on the streets any animal still with paws enough to stand upon began to run. And that is all they did: they ran.

Dogs. Cats. Foxes. All mad with fright, all sick with grief, they ran. Followed the running paws in front of them. In frenzy, in panic, blind Bryna found herself leading the way with Kim pounding at her heels, needing to escape from what she – what they had all been a part of. And make no mistake, they had all been a part of it, had engineered it; and though perhaps none of them could have foreseen the dreadful scale of events, the responsibility belonged as much to the animals as it did to the men, the perpetrators of the final, most brutal act of violence.

Wasn't Skrinkle's death justification enough? Hadn't the worst of all their enemies indeed done battle? Wasn't that what Bryna had wanted, wasn't that what dead Ki-ya had asked of them?

The animals ran away . . .

The green lorry lurched to a stop. It had only reached the outskirts of the town, but it wasn't going any farther. Green metal men spilled out, shouting and screaming blue murder. In front of them heavy plumes of black smoke, red and blue sheet flame twisted angrily across the sky.

"What the . . . what the blo . . . what the blo . . ." Jock could not believe his eyes. "The stupid beggars have only gone and blown half the town to bits. And what the hell's this—?"

"Animals! Dogs and cats *again*! Masses of 'em," cried Coots, "coming right at us. And look! Ruddy foxes, too!"

Instinctively he raised his gun to his shoulder and fired as terrified animals hurled themselves towards him. His first magazine was empty before Smithie could stop him. "Heh, Coots, man, what do you think you're doing?"

"Just look out there for yourself, Smithie – it's a plague!"

"Never mind them. Can't you see they're scared stiff? We came here looking for looters, not to have a go at the local wildlife—"

"Aye, well, there aren't any looters, are there? Not live ones anyhow — Not unless cats and dogs have been taking their driving tests!"

In front of them, the animals had stopped in their tracks. Too stricken with fear to run on, or to turn and run away.

"Ha ha, very funny," said Jock, sarcastically. "Come on, let's get out of here, before those ruddy jet fighters come back and decide to take a pot shot at us."

"Hang about though — You know, I've seen some of these animals before. That funny-looking tortoiseshell . . . the blind beggar. She was one of them at the wire when we bagged those two moggies. And that mongrel, too – that old black bag of bones!" Smithie lifted his lucky crate down from the back of the lorry. "I think they're sort of pals, like."

"You gone barmy or summat, what do you think you're doing now? You're not letting them cats out, are you?"

"Just give me a minute, eh? There's nowt

else we can help with here, is there? And you said it yourself, Jock, we can't keep 'em forever. So if I'm right about that cat then this is as good a place as any to get ourselves rid."

Slowly, Smithie carried his wooden crate into the middle of the road, placed it there, as close to Bryna as he dared. He carefully knelt down and lifted the lid – hesitated a moment – and then eased the contents out on to the ground.

Even through her fear, Bryna sensed his gentle movements, but only expected some new kind of weapon, some new way of killing.

There was no understanding men. It wasn't a weapon. It was cats. Two fat cats, stretching their limbs and squealing with the pain of it, as if they had not done so for a very long time.

"Go on then, bugger off," Smithie whispered softly. "Bugger off before I change my mind and decide to shoot the lot of you myself."

"Smithie – are you coming? We can't hang around here all day!" yelled Coots. The engine of the lorry growled into life.

"Aye man, aye—" Smithie stood up, gave the cats a push with the bottom of his boot, turned and walked away.

"Treacle . . . ?" mewed Bryna hesitantly, as the cat's scent reached her nose, as the man's receded. "Treacle, is that really you?"

"Bryna? Oh, Bryna – yes. Yes, it is."

"Yes, it is, Captain," echoed the cat at Treacle's side, just like – just like Lugger always did . . .

Twenty-Three

Tail Ends

Bryna, Kim, Dart, Treacle and Lugger sat quietly together upon the open fields of the Town Moor, content to nurse their wounds; simply to be in each other's company. They ignored the inquisitive calling of cats, and the answering howls of dogs, who continued to creep out of secret hiding-places deep within the town, discovering themselves suddenly free.

Kim found himself looking up at the strange new skyline of the town, and he puzzled over it. After all the carnage, the devastation, why shouldn't the town appear different? Flames from the fires were still licking at the early morning sky, though less fierce now; their damage was done and they would die soon. But there was something else about the scene, something that had nothing to do with burning fires, and he wanted to make sense of it.

And then, he suddenly realised what it was . . . The sky *behind* the flames had changed colour. No longer blue, not the hard acid blue it had been for ever and a day. But a kind of grey, a deepening, turbulent, rolling grey . . . The grey of gathering clouds.

Clouds!

At Kim's side, blind Bryna began to purr contentedly; her soothing voice reaching out across the Moor, across the town, bringing a new calm there. And then, dog and cat together, they felt the first light drops of rain . . .